AFTER MIDNIGHT
RICHARD E. DAVIS

This book is a work of fiction, and except in the case of historical fact and/or geographical areas, any resemblance to actual persons, living or dead, is purely coincidental.

Copyright © Richard E. Davis 2023

This book is sold subject to the condition that it shall not, by way of trade or otherwise, be lent, resold, hired out, or otherwise circulated without the publisher's or writer's prior consent in any form of binding or cover other than that in which it is published and without a similar condition, including this condition, being imposed on the subsequent purchaser.

Cover design by Richard E. Davis
Typeset in Times New Roman
Published by Dimensions Beyond Media. All rights reserved.
Printed by Ingram Spark

I recently celebrated (if you would call it that) my 60th birthday; hitting that number caused some deep reflection, especially concerning *THIS* set of stories. The tales in this collection span the period from my teenage years to the present; each of them holds a place very near and dear to my heart.

ESPECIALLY the hay bale trilogy.

Written at the tender age of 16, it came to life when I saw an open field of those pesky rolling things, and my mind lurched sideways…and my first thought was…*WHAT IF?*

And so, killer hay bales were birthed into existence.

My friends, I give you this compilation of shorts…if you're able to smile through some, laugh at others, and afterward think, "Man, this guy is *out there*!"…that is exactly the reaction I'm hoping you'll have.

So, when it gets dark, and noises are amplified, and things go bump in the inky blackness; well, honestly, there is no better place to be…than under the covers, reading this book, safe in your bed…

…after midnight.

To my long-suffering wife, Jeannie. She puts up with my wild imagination; my quirks; my java addiction; and my incessant need to wear my headphones to drown out all the distractions of the world while I write.

She might say...including her.

But, I am indeed so thankful for her in many, many ways.

She has continually inspired me in my craft; pushing me to go farther; think bigger; and build better worlds.

And I would think that I'm a better writer, and maybe even a better person, because of it.

I love you, my precious angel.

AFTER MIDNIGHT

ATTACK OF THE KILLER HAY BALES

Richard E. Davis

AFTER MIDNIGHT

"C'mon, man...hay bales don't just come to life."
                    Anonymous dead person

Richard E. Davis

They watched…
and they *waited*.

Patiently they continued their vigil. It didn't matter how long they would have to sit there. They knew that they had all the time in the world.

Long ago, they had begun to realize what was happening to them. Long before the time of the modern-day combine and the automatic hay baler. Long before bucking hay meant good paychecks for hundreds of small-town farm boys.

Yes, they were bitter.

Bitter for revenge.

They wanted revenge for the countless times that their compatriots were fed to the cows—no matter that they had never been allowed to speak in their defense. And no matter that they had been slaughtered just like the Jews during Hitler's regime of terror.

And now, it was finally time. Time to show these poor humans what the word stampede was all about.

For many years they had sat, silent and afraid, without any guidance. But those days were finally over. Now, at last, they had the balls to do something about it.

It was time for…The Attack.

Another typical hot, sticky day in southeast Georgia. Temperature well into the nineties with no chance of rain. Heat baking off the pavement like a well-done pot roast.

Carl James shut off his tractor and rubbed a grimy hand across his face, surveying the dusty land before him. *Not much of a crop this year*, he thought dismally. *Corn even looks pathetic.*

The only thing that looked halfway decent were the newly rolled bales of hay that sat brooding over in the northwest field. Three hundred and seventy this year—pretty good, and plenty to feed his livestock until springtime.

James was mounting the tractor again when something caught his eye. Puzzled, he turned back in the direction of the bales. There was something different over there, but he just couldn't quite—

Yes, there it was. And it was indeed strange. It seemed almost as if the hay had…moved a little bit toward him. Instead of being jammed up against the fence, they now looked as if they had spread themselves all over the field.

"What in the hell is going on?" he muttered to no one in particular.

Except, maybe, the hay bales.

Mike King slammed on his brakes a touch too late. The Mustang he was hot-rodding skidded, almost slid into the ditch, and then reluctantly gave up the chase. King cleared the cobwebs out of his head. "Man, I ain't believing this!"

Right in front of his car, almost close enough to touch, hundreds of huge hay bales were nonchalantly crossing the road as if on a Sunday drive. They rolled from the general direction of the Simpson place, making a beeline for what appeared to be nowhere.

Nowhere except—

Holy cow, Mike realized. *They're headed towards town!*

King slammed his car in reverse and quickly glanced over his shoulder.

One monstrous bale was blocking his path.

And coming directly at him.

He didn't even have time to scream before it crushed him and his car.

Clear Lake—just another small town surrounding the bigger burg known far and wide as Waycross. A couple of downtown stores, the post office, and the local café, Eddie's Eats, were its' only claim to fame. Most of the locals farmed, and there were those few who preferred to commute the twenty-mile round trip to Waycross to work.

A nice, sleepy, peaceful little town.
Until today.

Sheriff Ralph Casper was wolfing down his usual after-lunch, pre-supper snack at one o'clock when he got—the call.

"What? Car wreck out on 301? Yeah, I got it. I'll be out there in a few minutes." He hung up the phone and turned to the shop's owner, Eddie Nesbaum. "Got another smash-up out on the highway," he drawled. "See ya later, Ed."

"Don't get too hungry while you're out there," Nesbaum joked.

Casper only grunted as he walked out.

"Heaven help us," Casper breathed.

He had driven his way out to the accident at normal speed, thinking all the while that it was one of those fender-benders that took more time to write up the reports than anything else. However, nothing could have prepared him for the grisly sight that now lay before him.

Mike King's convertible Mustang had been smashed as if a steamroller had run over it.

Twice.

Nothing discernible remained of the inside except for a crumpled corpse. A dark pool of what Casper could only guess was blood and other visceral matter seeped out from underneath the remains.

The sheriff's gorge rose slowly. In all the years he had been in law enforcement, this was undoubtedly the worst wreck he had ever seen.

"Oh, man…I wonder what could have caused this?"

He heard a slow, steady sound from behind, building in intensity until it reached an ear-splitting crescendo. He whirled around and caught a fleeting glimpse of a group of mammoth hay bales thundering down on him.

Casper had time to fire off two useless rounds from his .38.

And then he, too, was gone.

Now they had tasted blood.

And found that they liked it *very* much.

So on the bales rolled, gathering up more and more of their neighbors and friends as they rolled inexorably towards town. They numbered nearly one thousand now.

A huge, ominous dust cloud followed the hay, filling the sky with choking darkness.

And it seemed to be laughing.

Carl James thought that his hunch had been right. The hay bales, as crazy at it seemed, were indeed moving. He could see them off in the distance.

James was brave, having served both in the Army and Navy, but he sure wasn't a fool. He stayed safely hidden in the cornfield, away from the menacing horror unfolding before him. And, like so many others witnessing the phenomena, he simply could not believe that it was happening.

Someone has to know what's going on, he decided, and signed his own death warrant.

It was about a fifty-yard dash to the barn, where there was an extension on his phone. The way he had it figured, he could get there in plenty of time without the bales seeing him.

That's what he got for thinking.

He hopped out of the corn and made a mad dash for the security of the double barn doors. But being almost sixty years old, he just didn't move quite as fast as he used to.

And, unfortunately, that was where the two bundles of hay were lying in wait for him.

It was all over very quickly.

"Something's very wrong around here," Tim Daniels decided, which was a big understatement.

He had been cruising along Highway 301 when he happened upon the gruesome discovery the sheriff had also uncovered. But Casper, unlike Daniels, had displayed very bad timing.

The bales were long gone now, still on a collision course for Clear Lake. Daniels could see the huge path that they had sheared off on either side of the roadway. It appeared as if a small army convoy had driven through the underbrush.

"There's only one way to find out what's going on," mused Daniels as he foolishly threw his truck into four-wheel drive and tore down the trail after the bales.

The amount of destruction he was following was incredible. Whole trees were uprooted, thrown to the side just as a careless child might toss his toys around. Deep ruts covered the path, and his small Ford truck was pushed to the limits of endurance. The young man was amazed at the continual carnage.

After about five minutes of open-mouthed driving, Daniels spotted the dust cloud a quarter-mile ahead of him. He thought he could just make out some dimly lit shapes rolling down the countryside.

"What the—" Daniels squinted harder at the distant caravan, and suddenly his foot slammed down hard on the brake pedal at the same time as his head cracked painfully against the front windshield.

"Those are friggin' hay bales!" he gasped. "Friggin' hay bales!!"

His voice rising towards a scream, he slung his truck around and got the hell out of there.

Clear Lake was deathly quiet. Not a car moved on Main Street. All the store owners and customers had gathered in a small group outside of the post office, their attention drawn to the quickly darkening skies to the west of town.

"Whaddaya think it is, Frank?" This from the postmaster, Fred Streeper.

Frank Chapman shook his head. "Dunno, Fred… Looks like some kind of storm brewing up."

"If it is, it's one of the weirdest that I've ever seen," the local grocer and part-time weatherman, Paul Aikerman, said. "Looks kinda like a dust storm."

There were numerous murmurs of agreement as they continued to watch the ominous sight build.

And the bales moved closer…

The time of reckoning was almost at hand.

Daniels drove his truck down the highway like a man possessed. He could think of only one thing to do, and that was to get back to town as quickly as he could and see if anyone could help him sort out this crazy mess. *Maybe*, he thought, *someone else sees what's going on and called the sheriff.*

He pushed the speedometer needle past eighty and kept it climbing. The sooner he got back to Clear Lake, the better. Anything to get away from the horror back there.

But he didn't know that the horror was just beginning.

At last, they had made it.

Over two thousand and fifty-eight hay bales now surrounded the entire city of Clear Lake. Small ones; big ones; monstrous round ones and even square ones that had been pushed forward by their larger cousins.

They sat silently around this small Georgia town, forming an impenetrable wall of straw. No one could get in; no one could get out. It was that simple. They had waited for eons for this moment, and they simply would not be denied success. They had planned well.

A hot, dry wind blew across the cornfields. It whispered of *hope*.

And the bales patiently waited.

The townspeople knew.

They too had gathered together, hurriedly discussing their options, which at the moment were few. For once, mankind had been stuck between the proverbial rock and a hard place, and the squeezing had begun in earnest.

"What are we gonna do?" Streeper pleaded, his face a ghostly white.

"Looks like we'll have to stick it out and wait," Aikerman decided. "After all, what choice do we really have? They've got us blocked in from all sides. We sure can't run for it…we'd be toast."

"I wonder what they want?"

Aikerman barked out a bitter laugh. "Maybe they don't want anything…except to kill us all."

"But why? My God, what have we ever done to them?" Streeper wanted to know.

"Maybe, just maybe…they want revenge."

Tim Daniels had finally reached Clear Lake.

But it was too late.

The bales were everywhere, cutting off the town from any kind of help. Over the tops of the bales, Daniels could see the townspeople knitted together, discussing something just out of earshot.

Frustrated, he closed his eyes and bumped his head against the steering wheel. So close, and yet so damn far. How in the world was he going to help them out?

The fire engines, his mind gently prodded. *They carry gasoline in the back for emergencies.*

Gasoline. He could set the hay on fire! All they would do then was burn themselves out. It was the perfect plan.

Or so he thought.

Daniels raised his eyes and saw the volunteer station, and the lone engine that sat parked out front. Three large bales stood guard, silently beside it. But a little to the right was a space that appeared just big enough for his truck to slip through.

The key word was *appeared*.

"Well, you ain't going to get nowhere in life sittin' on your ass, dude," he muttered, a crazy grin forming on his face. He very gently eased the truck into gear and mashed down on the gas pedal.

The hay had been expecting this move. Four more huge bales rolled out from behind the fire station and made a beeline for his vehicle just as he opened his door and flung himself out.

The moving monsters descended upon the hapless Ford pickup as it smashed into the lower part of the fire engine and burst into flames.

There was instant chaos.

Fiery bales trundled across the open expanse, ignited the others, and suddenly a sheet of flames ringed the town. To Daniels, it sounded as if they were screaming in intense pain and anguish. Flames jumped from bale to bale like a spreading wildfire. The hay was panicking; losing that one-mind consciousness that had carried them so far along on their mission.

Daniels picked himself off the ground and flung a fist into the blackened air, screaming in triumph.

And then the look on his face went from joy to absolute fear. The bales were moving again—this time right at the town of Clear Lake.

As they descended upon the unprepared city, the horizon was lit with what seemed like the world's largest bonfire. Daniels could only watch, stunned beyond belief, as the killer hay set fire to every single building and crushed the human opposition.

It was all over in less than five minutes.

And even though it meant that the hay had to perish, the bales had finally accomplished their lifelong goal.

Revenge.

Tim Daniels stood, weeping, along what used to be the outskirts of Clear Lake.

Everywhere he looked the bales had done their destruction.

And now, he was the only one left to tell the story. Insane as it might have sounded.

No, more like impossible. Who would ever believe him?

Man, no one will believe me, he thought. *They'll probably think I torched the town or something.*

So he stood there in silent reflection and watched the fires burn on.

And never heard nor saw the one last killer hay bale as it rolled up behind him…

The fires burned on.

Richard E. Davis

AFTER MIDNIGHT

THE SLOUGH

Richard E. Davis

AFTER MIDNIGHT

*"In the backwaters swirling, there is
Something that'll never change."*
　　　　"Backwater," Meat Puppets

Richard E. Davis

AFTER MIDNIGHT

The swollen globe of light broke free from the horizon, radiating blistering heat. Everywhere it touched insects, animals, and even people shied away from the muggy and oppressive summer warmth.

It was an unusually hot June in northern Missouri, and the weather pundits were calling for more of the same into August. "A heat dome" was the term they had coined for this rare phenomenon; most of the locals just called it darn hot.

Chariton County Sheriff Pete Carvel stepped out of his patrol SUV, took out a handkerchief, and wiped his brow furiously. "Damned hot is what I call it," he mumbled sadly.

At six-two and a buck ninety-five, Carvel was tall but not lanky; single and not looking. He was not your typical prototype sheriff, but he was no-nonsense, and everyone liked him because of it. He was resolutely dedicated to his job and put all his energy and resources into it each day. The women swooned over him, but his first love was fishing and the outdoors. He sometimes wondered if he would have been better suited as a conservation agent than a cop. But here he was, ten years into his stint as the top county hound dog, and he was content with life.

The sheriff replaced the damp cloth back in his pocket and turned his attention to the brackish waters in front of him: The Slough, as locals called it, was a backwater of Stanley Lake near Sumner, Missouri, population 102. The town's biggest claim to fame was the annual Wild Goose festival, which drew thousands of people for a time of drinking, debauchery, and deviant behavior over one weekend in late October. During the rest of the year, Sumner was just a small burg in search of bigger ideals.

Carvel scanned the still dark water for any kind of movement. Usually, during the morning hours, the popping and snapping of bluegills sucking in their latest meal was heard everywhere around this vast fishing hole; but this morning, even those noises were missing.

That's what worried the veteran policeman. It was way too quiet for his liking. It had been that way for most of the summer, too.

And, for two weeks straight, he and several other law enforcement officials had been scouring the surrounding countryside for a missing couple. Carlos Rivera and his pregnant girlfriend, Mindy Satchel, had just…disappeared. Their car was found abandoned on a nearby gravel road just a few hundred yards from the slough, doors open, and personal belongings inside. Nothing else…except a huge dent along the driver's door and front quarter panel, some scaly-like skin, and traces of blood. It appeared that a large fish had t-boned into the car, but there was no carcass to be found. And that was theory was more than stupid; it was downright idiotic. Yet, the couple had not been in touch with their friends and relatives for over fifteen days.

"Just another bit of weirdness," Carvel spoke out loud, breaking the morning stillness A flock of crows angrily squawked at him and took wing, circling a few times to scold the officer before heading north.

In the quiet that followed, Carvel was uneasy. He glanced around and suddenly noticed that besides the birds, there were no other sounds. No rustling animals, and no birds chirping their happy songs. The annoying cicadas buzzing their musical summer madness didn't even break the stillness.

And, again, there were no fish popping bubbles on the still, slightly oily, and brackish waters of the slough. It was puzzling.

And the utter, deafening silence didn't help.

The sheriff shuffled backward, never taking his eyes off the dark and inviting underbrush surrounding him. A chill ran down his spine as he intently peered into the blackness.

One step, then another slow, tentative move. Carvel's right hand automatically slid down and unlatched his gun holster, and he rested his palm gently on the comforting grip. The cool metal and tight wood handle gave him false confidence.

Another few feet back, he bumped into his vehicle abruptly. Carvel squeaked out a nervous sigh of relief and shook his head, chuckling to himself.

What are you scared of, man? The boogeyman?

However, he never took his eyes off the deep blackness of the timber as he got into his police cruiser, slammed it into gear, and flung gravel and dirt high into the air as he sped off.

Two days later.

Carvel sat in his office in the small town of Keytesville on a quiet mid-week late afternoon, going through last week's police reports. It was much of the same: two-bit teenage vandalism of dented, smashed mailboxes, stolen stop signs, and hurriedly discarded six-packs of cheap beer littering the area; numerous DUI arrests around the county from the usual drunkards; and a rather alarming stack of speeding tickets from one deputy in particular.

The sheriff sighed, then punched the phone intercom button. "Hey, Doris," he greeted. "Is Finch out there?"

His head dispatcher, Doris Englewood, a curvy and vivacious divorcee, answered back sweetly. "Hey, Pete. Yeah, he's sitting over at his desk filling out another speeding ticket report. You need him for something?"

Carvel rose from his desk and peered out his closed miniblinds. There was the young, arrogant, and pain-in-his-butt officer intently working on yet another one of his catches. *Boy, this is gonna be fun*, he thought humorlessly. "Yeah, go ahead and tell him I want to see him in my office as soon as possible, Doris. I need to discuss a few things with him."

Doris chuckled huskily, a bit of mischief in her voice. "Sure will, sheriff." A pause, and then, "we still on for this Friday night at the River Bottom Bar?"

Carvel shook his head as a gentle smile rose on his lips. *She sure doesn't forget anything*, he mused. "Yes, ma'am," he quickly answered. "I'll have to meet you there, though. Duty calls as always."

"Sounds good, Pete. I'll send the deputy right in."

A few moments later a brisk staccato knock as the door opened and Finch poked his head in. "Yeah Chief, what do you need?"

The sheriff gazed back wordlessly at Deputy Stanley Finch, a sure-of-himself S.O.B. if there was ever one. From his slicked-back dark hair to his 80's thick pornstache, he callously exuded what his mom used to call "arrogidence"—arrogance and confidence all rolled up into one big mess of a human being. *If someone ever thought their stuff didn't stink, it was this guy*, Carvel mused.

He let out an airless sigh and dove right in. "Finch, we need to talk about the stack of speeding tickets you've been issuing lately," the sheriff began, as Finch's shoulders straightened out in utter defiance; he pressed on. "I know that you want to do the best job that you can for the county, but there are many on the county commission and also some town council members that have been complaining about your lack of empathy and compassion. They wanted me to address it to you and see if we can figure something out."

"You're kidding me, right, boss?" The young man seemed incredulous. "I'm just out there upholding the law…and if it seems I hand out a lot of tickets, then maybe something should be done with the number of people who think it's ok to break the law."

A small chuckle escaped the sheriff's lips, and that made the deputy even more furious. "Regardless of what you think about our department here, Finch, most of us get along with our fellow officers, and we also try our best to be upstanding citizens of our communities and counties, while also being compassionate towards the needs of others. Yeah, some try to bend the law to suit their needs, but sooner or later it comes back to bite them hard." He shook a thick finger at the young man. "But...and I'm only gonna say this once: you going along half-cocked and antagonistic all the time is NOT in the best interests of the Chariton County Sheriff's Department. People are starting to talk, and the lowdown is that you need to get a handle on your arrogance and lack of compassion toward others and tone down your attitude a bit, young man...get my drift?"

The color quickly rose in Finch's cheeks. To Carvel, it appeared as if someone cinched up his neck and made a neat and taut red balloon on his shoulders. *Pennywise the clown*, he thought aimlessly as the Stephen King book came to mind, and the mental image made him laugh a little louder this time.

That made the situation worse; all the emotion suddenly drained out of Finch's face, replaced by a stony glare. "I get your drift, sir," he replied in a small thin voice. "Is that all?"

A very tight smile from Carvel was the only reply needed. With that, the deputy turned on his heels and stormed out of the office. A few moments later, the slam of a back door and squealing of a patrol car's tires. Then, blissful silence.

Doris's face slowly peered around the office door. "Everything ok, Pete? Finch looked madder than a wet hen when he left!"

"Yeah, he'll get over it, and himself, soon enough," he decided. Carvel leaned back in his chair, propped his feet up on the desk, and laced his hands behind his head. "If this is the worst thing that is going to happen today, it's going to be a good day."

As he sped far away from the station, Finch was furious.

No, he was more than furious. He was *livid*.

To his overbearing, puffed-up mind, he was the only reason that Chariton County was on the road to recovery when it came to its' degenerate and immoral residents.

They were absolutely corrupt; prone to huge gaffes and irresponsible actions when it came to living a good and pure life. It was up to The Righteous Deputy to set them on the right path that would lead to their salvation from a lifetime of evil deeds. His momma had taught him well when it came to the Good Book and right living.

That was his train of thought as his foot mashed down on the accelerator, giving no mind to the vehicles that he was recklessly passing as he flew westbound on state Highway 139 toward his home in Sumner. The Ford Explorer Interceptor hit 95 mph and kept climbing as he tried to quell the anger welling up from deep inside his gut.

What a jerk, Finch mulled silently. *Carvel thinks he knows everything about being a good cop. Well, he doesn't have a clue because he never gets out in the field anymore. I sure could teach him a thing or two.*

He flung the wheel hard over as his tires vainly protested on the hot asphalt; then he was sliding back and forth on the gravelly roadbed of Lakeside Avenue as he increased his speed back up to a respectable 60 and held it there.

Ahead, the early evening sun threw blinding shafts of light across the windshield. Finch flicked his sunshade down and squinted against the glare just as a flash of brown and white ran out in front of the vehicle.

Finch screeched; a whispery sound that was barely heard above the crunch of gravel as the deputy overcorrected. The patrol car spun out wildly in the opposite direction, bounded off the guardrail once, then twice, finally flipping over with a loud *thump!*

and splashing down into the murky waters of the slough.

The deputy vaguely felt the warm liquid rapidly filling the vehicle; his face had impacted the steering wheel and the sting of blood made it hard to keep his eyes open. He fumbled with his seat belt, snapped it open, then pushed himself up and out of the mangled death trap.

Five feet above him, the sunlight glistened, a beacon of safety. He clawed his way up and up, the weight of his utility belt slowing his progress.

Finch broke free into the welcome sunlight and gulped in the fresh air. He glanced at the shore where a fresh-faced doe stood mute, inquisitively staring back at him.

Suddenly he felt a yank on his left arm and went under again, a horrible stinging pain exploding in his body as the waters around him turned red. Shocked, he brought his arm up to his face and saw a huge gash, with muscles and tendons exposed. Bubbles exploded around him as he exhaled and continued pushing on.

He broke to the surface again, spitting and sputtering but thankful to be alive.

"What in the hell was that?" he shouted, holding his injured arm to his chest while treading water with the other. Around him, the waters continued to flow a dark red as his lifeblood slowly emptied out.

"Got to get to dry land and get some help," he muttered around the pain. "But by God, this *hurts*!"

His thoughts trailed off as he suddenly spied a surge of water circling from deep within the slough. It appeared to be the trail of a huge fish.

Finch continued clumsily treading water as the anomaly turned and swam closer; seventy-five feet; then fifty; then thirty…and at that distance, a distinctive form emerged from the swells that made him scream again with full-throated fear. He clumsily paddled around and headed towards the nearby shoreline.

As it closed rapidly in on him, there was a fleeting glimpse of thick reptilian skin flashing on the underside of the beast, with massive pointy teeth stretched wide apart, ready to devour.

And those eyes.

Oh my God, those eyes, he mindlessly mouthed.

Horrible, glowing green eyes full of evil.

The final sound in Deputy Finch's pathetic life was a tiny *urk!* as he was yanked down into the dark liquid. Tumultuous bubbles rose to the surface as the waters blossomed crimson red, then rippled in and out…in and out…dying rings that drifted farther out into the body of the slough until all was still again.

Beep! Beep! Beep! Beep!

The shrill backup warning from the tow truck was grating on Sheriff Carvel's nerves; first, he had the beginnings of a headache, and second, now he was missing that fart-faced deputy, Finch.

And, to top it all off, said officer's patrol car was now being dragged out from the slough, inch by muddy inch.

"Chief!" his second-in-command, Lt. Matt Stormington, yelled from the shore. "We got something here!"

"What is it, Matt?"

"It looks to be…oh my God." The heavyset senior member of the Chariton County Sheriff's Department promptly turned and lost his lunch in the underbrush. After a few moments, he wiped his mouth with a shaking arm. "Pete, you need to get down here, pronto." He pointed into the vegetation.

Carvel clambered down the steep bank and strode over to Stormington. He turned his eyes to what his deputy had seen, and the gorge rose quickly. "Oh, man. What in the hell is this?"

There, partially hidden in the thick growth, was a partially decomposed, half-eaten, but readily recognizable man's torso wearing a tattered Grateful Dead t-shirt.

The sheriff slowly approached the rotting flesh as a cloud of flies buzzed angrily in protest. And then the smell hit him.

That odor was something that never escaped his memory. It was fetid; noxious; the kind of stench that one associated with bloated roadkill on a hot summer day; a smell that would infiltrate the nostrils and stubbornly cling to the interior of passing cars as if trying to hitch a ride to more aromatic venues.

Swallowing the bile that threatened to escape his mouth, Carvel pushed forward, waving aside the flies. He took out his Maglite and flicked it on while also drawing his gun in one smooth motion. Both the Glock 9mm and the high-intensity beam played over the ghastly scene as he swept them from left to right.

Stormington joined him, even as his stomach protested the move. "Oh, man, Pete…is that Rivera?"

Carvel nodded even as he continued to study the body. "From the description we got from his friends, I would have to say so, Matt." He knelt, took out a pen, and lifted the ripped shirt. There, right above his left pectoral, were the tattooed words Mindy's Heart.

"Yeah, that's him, all right," Stormington concurred. "Recognize the ink from the pics we gathered. Jeez, Pete, what in the blazes happened to him? It looks like he's been chewed up by something!"

The senior officer shook his head as he holstered his pistol; a twinge of fear struck a dagger in his heart. "I don't know, man." He stood up and gazed at the remains, and then stared long and hard at the slough. "Could've been a bear, maybe coyotes…a stray mountain lion, or maybe even feral dogs. But there haven't been any bear sightings around here for a long, long time." He continued his furtive study of the surrounding waters. "One thing I know, though. This is now officially a crime scene. We'll have to get State Patrol's help with this one."

Both men looked again at the calm and peaceful waters. The slough had always been a place of refuge for the community; not only a great fishing hole, but a social gathering spot for picnics, bbqs, and much more. Now it was a grim harbor of death and despair.

And the worst was yet to come.

Missouri State Trooper Sgt. Ted "Buddy" Jacobsen was a 35-year veteran of the Highway Patrol and had a long and industrious career; he currently served as the head of the Division of Drug and Crime

Control, the investigative branch of the Criminal Investigation Bureau. He was also best friends with Chariton County's sheriff; and when he received the call about a crime there, he hightailed it to the scene the next morning. Jacobsen came trundling up to the scene, two cases filled with forensic testing equipment in his hands.

"I would say good to see you again, my friend," Jacobsen stated, "But under the circumstances, I can see why it's not time for a fishing reunion trip."

Carvel wanly smiled. "Yeah, that's my thought as well, Buddy." They were both standing over the body, yellow tape zigzagging through the crime scene. "You got any thoughts on this craziness?"

His trooper friend let out a long sigh, and then turned and gazed at the slough waters. "Dunno, Pete. I'm at a loss for words right now." He reached down, scooped up a flat rock, and sent it skimming across to the opposite bank.

Plop!
Plop!
Plop!
PLINK!

That last sound caused everyone to turn. There, on the far shoreline was a glint of metal, twinkling in the early morning sunlight. The two of them jogged over to see what Jacobsen's aim has uncovered.

Sheriff Carvel bent down, and with one gloved hand slowly brushed away the mud and muck around the object, then picked it up: a severed and mangled hand gripping an open pocketknife, the blade wedged into a clump of huge, glistening armored scale-like material.

"What in the hell?" Buddy Jacobsen muttered around clenched teeth.

Carvel slowly spun the knife around, revealing chunks of wet, greenish fish-like meat. Thin tendrils of blue veins dangled from the mass, oozing out a thick black substance as it pulsed weakly, in and out…in and out.

And the smell was rancid and cloying; like Death itself had invaded every pore and orifice of their bodies. A few of the deputies stumbled away gagging.

Carvel reached into his back pocket with his free hand, retrieved a handkerchief, and clamped it to his nose. He could almost taste the foulness surrounding him. "Buddy, you got an evidence bag handy?"

Jacobsen nodded. "Yeah, Pete." He looked around and pitched his voice louder. "Hey, can someone get me a bag to put this crap in please?" He felt waves of nausea pour over him; and for a fleeting moment, he felt lightheaded. He had served for decades in law enforcement and never had experienced a crime scene like this.

A comforting hand dropped onto the trooper's shoulder; it was Carvel. *Thank God for small favors*, he thought.

"You ok, bud?" It was phrased as a question, but both men knew that it was something more; an affirmation of the absolute dread everyone felt by this sudden turn of events.

Jacobsen nodded as he opened an evidence bag and solemnly watched Carver deposit the severed part and its contents into the plastic. "Uh-huh." His voice was shaky and uncertain. "Just never thought I'd see anything like this, man." He sealed the bag shut and placed it in an iced-down cooler, then viciously scrubbed his hands against his pants leg. The filth and disgust were evident on his face: he managed a weak croak before apologetically looking at his friend. "Sorry, Pete. This is just...weird."

"No worries, Ted." Carver seldom uttered his real name. "I think it's pretty hard on all of us." He thought for a few moments, then in a very small voice stated the obvious. "I think it's time to bring the divers in and see what else we can find."

Both of them stood silently, each lost in their own thoughts.

Overhead, the clouds began to thicken, and faint thunder rolled in the distance.

Later that afternoon, the rain began to fall.

It started slowly and gently, cascading in sheets from the swollen, dirty sky. As the thunderstorms matured into full-blown supercells in just a few hours, the skies unleashed a full-throttle downpour, overflowing the antique sewers in Sumner, Brookfield, and much of the surrounding area. Streets were submerged; underpasses shut down; and a general muddy mess ensued.

Carver sat alone in the cop shop as the rain lashed against the windows and the lights flickered ominously. He nervously glanced at his watch; they had been making regular checks on the electric substation since the deluge started, and the water was already lapping at the doors. If the rains continued, the pumping systems were at risk of being submerged; if that happened, then the power grid would cascade into a complete shutdown for much of northern Missouri.

The weather forecast for the next day or two was troubling as well, with continued downpours, areal flood watches and warnings, and an overall mess becoming more and more likely.

He glanced at the phone again; he was expecting a call from the local medical examiner concerning a preliminary result from the autopsy of Carlos Rivera's body. But the receiver lay in its cradle, mute and unforgiving.

"Sonofa—" Carver began, then bit his tongue as his voice started rising. *No need to get anyone else all frazzled about this, man*, he quietly admonished himself. *Better to keep it close to the vest for now.*

His mind was racing on many different levels; he felt like he was in the middle of one of his nephew's favorite old games, Super Mario Cart, and the bad guys were not only chasing him, they were quickly pummeling him into submission and a last-place finish.

What in the hell was eating on him? That thought kept tumbling around in his head, and it was a disturbing one. Rivera's flesh had been not only been chewed on; devoured would be a better word for the tangled mess that was left for them to find. There was no doubt about that one inescapable conclusion.

Coupled with that was the tooth that they had found; or better yet, the prehistoric incisor that was indicative of something sinister that was lurking somewhere in the muddy waters of the slough. Just those unspoken words were enough to raise the hairs on the nape of the sheriff's neck.

Another thought rose in Carver's mind, and that was from a long-ago chat he had accidentally overheard between his grandfather and one of his war buddies. The scuttlebutt was that there was some kind of underground cave system that linked the slough to the old abandoned coal mines that were littered throughout the area; mine shafts and caverns that twisted, turned, and ran for hundreds, if not thousands, of feet.

Or maybe even miles. No one had ever found the end of the tunnels.

And, there were the disappearances. Dozens of missing coal miners and children; hundreds of vanished farm animals. Nine times out of ten, the bodies had never been found.

And half of the towns around here are sitting right on top of the friggin' things, Carver thought, and at that moment, the phone shrilled violently. He jumped, then nervously laughed at his stupidity as he picked up the receiver. "Carver here," he barked.

Local coroner Ben Harvey's voice floated tinnily through the crackling phone lines. "Hey, Sheriff, just got finished with the autopsy." There was a long pause, and Carver sensed that the man was struggling to find the right wording to say. "And what I found is very… puzzling."

Carver drew in a long breath. "Puzzling?"

"Yessir, to say the least. I think it's better if I come on down to the station and we can have a face-to-face about the results. I'm at a loss for words on what I discovered." Harvey's voice trembled a bit. "I think we might have a really big problem here."

"OK," Carver conceded. "I'll be here for a while, monitoring the flooding situation. Hightail it out here as soon as you can."

"Will do, sir." The line went dead.

An hour and a half later, the sheriff was flummoxed.

He leaned back in his chair after Harvey finished his proclamation and stared off into space for a few long moments, absorbing everything that he had just heard.

Finally, Carver spoke in wavering tones. "That… that's just not possible, Ben," he managed to blurt out. "What you're telling me borders on insanity."

Harvey nodded. "I know it does, Sheriff. But the evidence doesn't lie." He threw up his hands. "I did the bloodwork, the examination…everything, including the specimen that was retrieved from the deceased. And there's only one conclusion I can come up with."

"That some kind of reptilian prehistoric beast killed Rivera?" the law officer finished. "Ummm, no. Here we go with that crazy talk of the Dark Dunkie. I can't believe that stupid fairy tale, man. It flies in the face of—"

"Of science? Of real life?" The coroner gazed uncomfortably at Carver for several moments until the sheriff dropped his eyes. "Trust me, I know how crazy this all sounds. But science doesn't lie. Something is out there, and it attacked and most likely killed and ate both Rivera and Satchel. Her body hasn't turned up yet but if it did…we would see the same kind of biological evidence on it as well. The tooth from Rivera proved that; after consulting with some of my colleagues, it appears to have definitive reptilian characteristics. Almost like a hybrid between a land-walking mammal and some kind of ancient fish."

"How can you explain that, doc? Sounds like some sci-fi crap from a bad B movie." Carver chuckled half-heartedly.

Harvey shrugged. "I can't Pete; or at least, I can only give you what the facts point to: that something is going on here that transcends our current understanding. It's disturbing, to say the least. All I can say is that we have some kind of new species, or a major evolution of a prehistoric species, living in the slough's waters. It may very well be responsible for the deaths of Carlos Rivera and Mindy Satchel. And… maybe even others who've disappeared from around here."

The sheriff stared long and hard at Harvey; the seconds stretched into a minute of deafening silence, then two. He broke the stillness in a thin and hesitant voice. "Thanks, Ben. Looks like I may need to call in some major help before it gets any worse."

"I think the worse has already gotten here, Pete," the coroner deadpanned with a worried look on his face.

And outside, the rain continued its relentless torrent.

Three hours later the power died with a bang.

Four transformers lit up the late afternoon sky with enormous blue balls of fire as the water overwhelmed the power company employees' best sandbagging efforts. Grid by grid, residents and businesses alike were thrust into power-sapping oblivion.

Carver was in the middle of an urgent phone call with his friend Buddy Jacobsen when the connection terminated and his office was plunged into darkness. "Crap!" he cursed violently and flung the handset across the room. "What else is gonna go wrong?" He fumbled around in the dark for a few moments, then scooped up his keys and splashed out the door.

It swam on and on.

Dunkleosteus was its former name, from the genus *arthrodire placoderm*; a huge, armored meat-eating fish that weighed a little under one ton, measured twenty feet in length, and was equipped with a bite force of over twenty-thousand pounds per square inch.

A mean and muscular waterborne killing machine that had evolved into something more.

A fish with webbed feet and the ability to walk on land.

The armored hybrid mutant and its family had hastily retreated into the twisting maze of submerged caverns in northern Missouri during the mass extinction event of the Devonian period; and as the decades and centuries wore on, they were content to feed upon the hapless wild animals and pre-humans that dared to venture into their lair. Their numbers swelled to over thirty at one point during their evolutionary lifecycle, and during that time it had gained the ability to breathe and live on land as it successfully mated with a Dinogorgon. The offspring that followed thrived in both environments; however, as food become scarcer and eons passed, future generations resorted to cannibalism until there were only a few left.

This family ventured further and further out of the caverns of north Missouri until they found a small opening into a brackish backwater; with some difficulty they squeezed through and found a sanctuary of ample food and freedom. Livestock in the form of cows and pigs was everywhere; the occasional human (or two) working in the mines was also nice, and assorted other animals were there to help sustain their voracious appetites. However, over time, the remainder slowly died off until there was only a sole survivor.

That creature became the legend known as the Dark Dunkie; similar to the Loch Ness Monster, except with a name that resembled a donut franchise.

The surrounding area had no festival for it; no special celebration commemorating its existence…it was whispered about during late-night camping trips, or told to frightened children during ghost story time at sleepovers.

But it was real…and it was ticked off.

And as the rain continued falling and the runoff filled up the mineshafts, tunnels, and caverns, even more passages were being opened up for the monstrous beast to travel…with many more places for it to feed.

Ben Harvey was stuck.
Between a rock and a hard place.
Literally.
He had been cruising faster than normal along the flooded roadway in his Subaru Outback, when his right tire left the pavement. Harvey overcorrected and his vehicle slid sideways into the water-filled ditch, slamming up against a large boulder. After a few metal-screeching moments, the Subaru wedged itself against the rock and the concrete culvert.

Water began to fill the vehicle as Harvey hastily unsnapped his seatbelt and rolled down the driver's window. *Thank God for manual cranks*, he thought aimlessly as the lukewarm liquid engulfed the auto's interior.

Sputtering and coughing, Harvey clambered and clawed his way up the slick banks to the roadway. He gazed back just as the Outback gave up the ghost and disappeared into the floodwaters.

"There go my insurance rates," Harvey muttered, chuckling despite his circumstances. "Time for a long, wet walk back to town."

He felt warmth running down his left arm and glanced down, alarmed at the flow of blood oozing from a large gash. Unconcerned, he tore off a piece of his shirt and tied it just above the wound in a makeshift tourniquet, then began walking east on Highway 139 towards civilization. Just ahead, the town of Sumner beckoned him along.

And just behind him, a short dorsal fin slowly rose up and kept pace with Harvey as he sloshed up the roadway bridge, blood dripping from his arm and running off into the waters below him.

The leviathan smelled blood, and it was on the hunt.

Chariton County Sheriff Pete Carvel flew up Highway 139 like a madman, directing his officers via cell phone and radio at the same time. He was wrestling with the gut feeling that the area around the slough needed to be evacuated as soon as possible, and time was of the essence. He felt; no, the better term was he *knew* that as crazy as it sounded, the fish/monster/whatever the hell it was would strike again soon, given the fact that its feeding ground was exponentially expanding with the rain. Already, flood watches had been upgraded to areal warnings, and all the north-central part of the state could be underwater soon…which now meant the menu was about to be upgraded to an all-you-can-eat buffet of immense proportions.

Carver steadily pushed his foot to the floor as the car accelerated to 75, then 80. He could dimly see the slough bridge through the downpour, and a lone figure trying to flag him down.

Harvey was desperately waving his arms as he spied headlights in front of him. With a trembling finger, he squeegeed the pouring rain off his glasses as he furtively glanced in all directions. He had a distinct feeling that he was being…*watched.*

By what or whom, he couldn't say. The skin on the back of his neck was crawling, even through the warm dampness of the day as he broke out into a run towards the oncoming vehicle.

And then chaos ensued.

Carver was almost at Harvey's location when a monstrous finned figure exploded from the slough. Dimly, through the frenzy of the full-on windshield wipers, he saw Harvey slowly turn, a look of horror etched on his face, moments before he disappeared, screaming, into the belly of the beast.

The sheriff mashed the brake as the squad car hydroplaned through the mud and muck, aiming directly at Dunkie, who was now standing on the bridge and glaring at him with those cold, green optics.

As his patrol car smashed into the prehistoric beast, it let out an ear-piercing roar as its hide was split open; at the same time the windows shattered, peppering the law enforcement officer with glass shrapnel. He dimly felt tiny rivulets of blood begin oozing down his face and arms as he gratefully passed out from the impact.

Darkness. Water flowing.

A low-pitched growling.

Carver opened up his eyes slowly and painfully. He tried moving his legs, but they were pinned tightly between the seats and part of the engine that was now in the car's interior.

"Damnit!' he cursed, then stopped as he felt a cold and unrelenting fetid smell wafting across his face. He gingerly turned his head to the left.

Where he was met with two glowing green eyes filled with hate.

The Dark Dunkie wheezed its dying breath in and out…in and out; never taking those eyes off him. The monster studied him carefully, just as a kid would examine ants under a magnifying glass just before the scorched earth policy took effect. It was chilling and unnerving to Carver.

His eyes inched down to the leviathan's stomach, gashed open by the car's brute force. Steaming bluish intestines and bodily fluids spilled out into the car's interior; they were laced with large round nodules that glowed with a pulsating light.

Carver tried to breathe around the noxious smell, gagging uncontrollably. The Dunkie growled, then nudged him with his armored head. He felt razor-sharp teeth scrape across his cheek as he faced the menacing terror again.

Its eyes slowly dimmed, brightened once, then twice; then mercifully extinguished as the head dropped to the side.

The Dunkie was dead.

Sheriff Carver exhaled thankfully, then paused.

Yes, there it was again. A *sound*.

Like tiny whimpering.

He looked around, then down. And his eyes grew wide.

Among the creature's innards was a stirring. The round orbs were pulsating brighter, and there was movement within them…then gnashing noises, like teeth tearing into something.

One by one, tiny heads poked up out of the objects and looked at him.

Eggs. Oh my God, those are EGGS!

Carver tried to reach for his service pistol.

Unfortunately, it was just out of his grasp.

He had time for one last futile scream before they tore into him.

Richard E. Davis

CHAIN LIGHTNIN' (Part One)

Richard E. Davis

AFTER MIDNIGHT

*"It's chain lightnin', too hot to fight
Hot on the heels of a Saturday night
Chain lightnin' out of control
Straight to the heart and down to your soul."*
"Chain Lightnin'," 38 Special

Richard E. Davis

Steve Haverton was mad.

No…he was *PISSED*.

As he picked himself off the steaming black asphalt, the adolescent felt the familiar pain of gravel and glass embedding into his skin. And, as usual, the trickles of blood coursing down his chubby arms and legs. His glasses were askew. He felt a whimper start to bubble up, then wisely clamped it down. He didn't need any more torment this afternoon.

"Look at his fat ass, guys!" Ray Campbell shouted excitedly. "He can't even get up! And he's pissing himself!!"

The others bent over in laughter. This group of juvenile delinquents called themselves The Pack; young thugs masquerading as innocent kids attending Irving Middle School in Norman, Oklahoma. It seemed as if their whole purpose was bent on causing mayhem and madness where and when they could find the opportunity.

"Poor, poor Stevie baby…he fell down and wet his pants again," Ray continued. "D'ya need some help, sir?" He extended a hand.

Steve began to gingerly stand up, just as his nemesis yanked the hand back, causing the overweight youth to topple over again.

"Ahahaha!" The laughter rippled around him. Steve kept his head down so they wouldn't see the tears welling up in his eyes. He felt defeated and alone; an outcast among his classmates.

And that was his life, every moment of every day.

From the minute he woke up to the sounds of his parents screaming at each other, to the daily needling, ribbing, and bullying he endured at school, to the endless nights of tv dinners and homework and then listless sleep...well, that was the story of Steven Haverton.

Freak.

Loser.

Fat ass.

There were many other names that he was called, but those were the most hurtful; they seared his soul, slammed his psyche, and shamed his self-worth. If words were explosives, those three were the nukes that incinerated his inner world every time he started to rebuild it.

So he knelt there, his knees and hands baking impressions into the blacktop on an unseasonably hot April day, and sobbed uncontrollably.

Evening.

AFTER MIDNIGHT

After two Banquet Hungry Man country-fried chicken meals and a two-liter of Pepsi to wash them down with, Steve performed his nightly ritual: easing his upstairs window open, climbing out, and sitting on the roof. This was the only time when he felt at ease; staring off into the night sky, watching the crackling light show from late spring thunderstorms. The bolts of lightning danced as they arced across each cloud top and sizzled to the ground below.

The young man sighed and eased onto his back. His joints not only ached from the beating that he endured that afternoon, but also from all the excessive weight that he carried around constantly.

Yeah, the beating, he thought aimlessly.

His mom and dad were furious when he arrived home, clothes tattered and spotted with blood, snot, and urine. After the requisite interrogation, his mom Susan had threatened to call Ray's parents *AND* the police. It was only after several tense minutes that she had backed off, but she still looked at him painfully as he recounted the incident.

When all was said and done, Steve was on the butt end (which he thought was a terrible choice of words from his dad James) of not only a tongue-lashing, but also a grounding from all after-school activities.

And what was that going to do? The Pack would just hunt him down one way or another, and subject him to more rounds of fists, shoves, etc. then exit stage left when a teacher came running.

"Hey, Steve." The voice floated up from below him, jarring his inner musings, and he gingerly sat up.

Tammy Bligh, a wistful redheaded, freckle-faced adolescent, stood in his backyard. She was Steve's best friend—hell, she was his only friend. Through thick and thin, she was always there with a smile, candy bar, or just her presence. When she was around, it would always cheer him up.

And for a time, his ongoing battle with The Pack and his parents and just life in general would fade into the background.

For that, he was thankful.

"Hey, Tam." His voice cracked, and she looked at him worriedly.

"You OK?"

Steve shrugged. "Yeah, I guess. Pretty bad beat down today." He studied her carefully. "Hope you weren't around for it."

"I saw." Those two words hung in the air for an era. "Didn't like it."

"Sorry you had to watch."

"Steve, don't say you're sorry. Don't ever say that." She genuinely cared, and it showed in her voice. "Anything I can do?"

Even through the pain, Steve grinned. "Beat 'em up?" He chuckled, and sore muscles poked him in protest. "Nah. Happens every day. Just try to avoid them."

Tammy nodded, then deftly climbed the tree next to the apartment building. In a flash, she was on the roof, sitting next to her friend. She patted his hand, then followed Steve's gaze to the distant flashing thunderstorms.

"Cool show tonight."

"Yeah," Steve replied. His mind was far away.

Tammy shifted and turned to her friend. "Got a question."

Steve glanced at her curiously. "Sure, Tam."

"Why doncha just sock that a-hole sometime? I know he'll pound you back something fierce…but it might stop him from doing it to you anymore." The look on her face told Steve she was dead serious.

"Think it'll work? I don't." He threw up his hands in frustration. "He'd prolly kill me."

"Nah, he won't," she rebutted. "His dad is a big shot in town, and he don't want his name looking bad."

A big shot in town. That was an understatement. Carl Campbell was the City Manager of Norman; and a third-generation one, too. He strutted his status around town like a mating season peacock. His family adored him, as well as most people in town. The Campbells were hardworking folks trying to make a difference in Ward One, and nothing would sully the family name more than a scuffle with lower-class scum like the Haverton clan.

"Maybe Ray needs a lesson," Steve whispered under his breath. His eyebrows furrowed down, and his lips drew tight. The menace on his face was real, and for just a moment, as Tammy glanced at her friend, she felt…scared.

The day after.
April 25, 2025.
Steve slinked his way toward the school building, furtively glancing around to make sure he wasn't being followed. The sweat poured off his brow and soaked his shirt quickly in the oppressive heat and humidity.

He drew closer to the doors. Two hundred feet; then one hundred; he was almost there where he could bask in the air-conditioned hallways and—
WHAP!

Suddenly he was on his knees and the stars were circling his head like birds seeking a welcoming branch.

No, they weren't birds; rather, it was The Pack that was menacingly encroaching on his bubble.

He felt the rage well up, an all-consuming fire of hatred and bitterness, and remembered the words that Tammy had told him: *why doncha just sock that a-hole sometime?*

With that thought echoing through his head, he felt himself stand unsteadily to his feet as he balled up his right fist and let it fly.

Crack!! His mark was true; Ray's face registered shock as Steve's hand forcefully connected to his jaw and the bully dropped to the sidewalk, blood trickling from his mouth.

The Pack scattered, shocked at this sudden turn of events. Excited voices suddenly fell silent as Steve knelt and started putting fists to face as he screamed in triumph.

"How d'ya like this, punk? Huh?! Ya like it? Want some more?? Bout time someone gave it back to ya!!" The punches continued unabated.

That is, until Stu Sullivan, Irving Middle School's science teacher, mercifully pulled him off his defeated foe.

Ray propped himself up on his elbow and looked dead at Steve with swelling eyes as he spat out blood. "This ain't over, fatty!" he growled. "Ya dead meat, ya hear me? DEAD meat!!"

Sullivan turned and escorted Steve to the principal's office.

The young man bent over in the rigid wooden chair, a smile on his face as he awaited his fate from the head dog. Two Norman law enforcement officers were milling about down the hall, casting a glance his way as they conversed in hushed tones with Sullivan.

Irving's no-nonsense principal, Robert Claysmith, calmly walked out of his office and stood over Steve. "Would you like to come in for a talk, Mr. Haverton?"

With a sigh, he followed Claysmith into his plush, well-appointed room. Numerous accolades and pictures were lining the walls, along with awards decorating the shelves. Steve looked at them with disinterest, then plopped himself into a chair facing the principal.

"So, Mr. Haverton," Claysmith began. "Looks like you were in an altercation with Ray Campbell again. Care to elaborate?"

Steve cleared his throat; what came out was just barely above a whisper. "I gave him back what he's been giving me."

"Gave back?"

"Yeah. I gave him a beatdown," Steve replied matter-of-factly. "He just had what was coming to him."

"Mr. Haverton. I understand that you've been in numerous fights with him, and others, in the past. But what you did today I can't condone." He stared at the youth. "Throwing a punch is one thing…violence is not the answer; we never allow it…and continuing to beat on someone when they are down is entirely unacceptable."

Steve felt the blaze starting to rise, and he pushed it down. What came out of his mouth was cold and cutting. "Unacceptable? He's beat the shit out of me time after time, and he gets away with it. You don't do nothin' about it."

"Mr. Haverton!" The head teacher's tone raised several notches, and he sternly looked at his charge. "You will watch your mouth in this office."

"So, it's okay when the City Manager's son beats a fat kid but not okay when he beats back?" His voice rose as well, and the color blossomed in his cheeks.

"It's not, sir." The finality in his voice made Steve realize that nothing would happen to his enemy. Yet again. He was protected by the school, by the law…by *everyone*.

"We need to talk about steps moving forward, Mr. Haverton," the principal continued after a beat. "Disciplinary action for both of you is needed. Mr. Campbell's father declined to press charges, so we do not need to involve the local authorities. However, since this happened on school grounds, this does involve us." Claysmith stood up and walked over to his window and looked out, then turned to Steve. "Your mom is on the way to come get you and take you home. You are suspended for five days. After this time we will meet again with you and your parents to discuss further action."

Late afternoon.

The hazy blue skies had given way to building clouds and heat, and the National Weather Center in Norman was advising on a major cold front that would be sweeping through the area in just a few hours, with possible severe storms and heavy rain. The air felt heavy with anticipation of abundant moisture.

Steve sat in his room with headphones on and music blaring, thankful for the respite. His mom had just blistered his backside with a metal coat hanger, but that wasn't the worst.

No, the worst would be in just a few hours when his father came home. Not one for mincing words, he would take the belt to him (*hard enough to bring up bruises*, his mind processed coldly) and slam home his "operating principles" with whip-like precision:

Take yer medicine like a big boy
SMACK!
Shut yer mouth and open yer ears
WHOP!
Don't be a stupid ass.
WHACK!

Words to live by for sure.

Steve didn't let it bother him, though. He would indeed "take his medicine like a big boy" and just detach himself from what was happening; over the years he had built a place deep within himself that he went to during these times; a place where he was safe from any kind of harm.

Physically, mentally, and emotionally.

He called it his sanctum; his personal holy of holies.

As he sat there, he glimpsed a flash of light from outside. He pulled off his headphones and stuck his head out the window just as the thunder rolled; a deep, gut-rattling growling that made him smile.

Steve climbed out his window and perched himself on the rooftop; to the northwest, low dark clouds were quickly churning towards his location as the squall line advanced, followed by a series of electrostatic discharges that zapped the ground below.

Closer they came…still closer. The lightning raced across the sky, hitting the power poles right across the street, and Steve felt exhilarated. The booming that followed was ear-splitting; he had the fleeting thought of *"that's what God prolly sounds like…"*

And then the lightning struck.

He felt; no, he *sensed* what was happening as over three hundred million volts coursed through his body not just once.

Or twice.

But three times as multiple bolts slammed into him with a deafening roar, one after the other. He smelled his hair being singed off in an instant. Dimly, from what seemed to be a million miles away, he saw his skin glowing bright blue as he yelled…but nothing came out of his mouth.

And then darkness mercifully claimed him.

Just two buildings down, Tammy watched out her closed window at her friend sitting on the roof, broadly smiling as the storms drew closer. Then, in one horrific second, he became engulfed in a huge ball of light for what seemed like an eternity.

She screamed as the glare finally subsided, followed by the immediate thunderclaps. Steve's lifeless body rolled off the second-floor rooftop and dropped to the ground below with a thud.

Her mom Janet came running into the room. "What's the matter, honey?"

"Stu...Stu...Steve just got hit by lightning, Mom! I think he's dead!"

Janet pulled her phone out and immediately dialed 911.

Red and blue lights flashing.
Sirens.

Emergency crews raced into the neighborhood and came to a screeching halt in front of the Vicksburg Village Apartments, a lower-income housing complex directly across from the school. A crowd was gathering even as the dense curtain of rain poured down from the skies. The lightning had since abated, heading southeast with the mesoscale convective system. But the damage that was left in its wake was extensive.

The EMTs and rescue crew ran up to Steve's body; there was extensive burning on his head and feet, the entry/exit locations of the fatal lightning strikes. His clothes were scorched in several places where they fused with his skin.

"Oh my God," the lead paramedic exclaimed. "This is bad."

"Yeah, Bill, it is." The second crew member shook his head sadly. "I've never seen someone hit by lightning this bad."

"No pulse. Starting CPR."

As the first technician reached down with clasped hands to begin compressions, a static discharge leaped from the corpse and threw him a few feet back. He shook his head and stood up, dazed and frightened.

"What the hell?"

"Everyone back!" One of the firefighters grabbed a metal rod from the truck as he pulled his gloves on, then touched it to Steve. Immediately, the metal flashed blue and the man's gloves began smoking. He threw them as well as the rod down; the metal was melted and black.

"Criminy!" was all he could say as the paramedics were able to finally begin working over the lifeless body. "What is going on?"

Steve's remains were transported to the morgue a few hours after the lightning strikes, where his mother and father ID'd him between tears and cursing.

Tammy begged her mom to allow her to go with Steve's parents so that she could see him. She didn't care what he looked like; she had been the last person to see him alive, and she knew in her heart that he would want her there.

As she slowly walked toward the cold chamber, she shivered, and not just from the freezing temperatures in the room. It was the fact that her friend had gone through a horrible death, and he didn't deserve it. No one did.

But especially Steve. He had been put down; pushed aside; cast away his whole life.

She reached out a trembling hand and placed it on his cold one. The tears started flowing unabated.

"I'm sorry, Steve," she began, then shook her head. A faint smile touched her lips. "But I always told you not to say that, and here I am doing it. Hope you've found some peace now."

His hand twitched underneath hers, and she screamed.

The coroner and his parents came running in. "What happened, Tammy?" his mother demanded.

"His hand…it *moved*."

"That's impossible, young lady," the medical examiner stated. "I pronounced him a few hours ago. There's no way that he—"

Steve's hand jumped again, and then a ragged intake of breath from his icy parted lips. His eyes slowly fluttered open.

Another scream, this time from his mother.

Steve Haverton lay motionless in the hospital bed, tubes and IV's intersecting his body at various points. The incessant beeping on the vital signs monitor was the only activity in the room; that, and the monotone regularity of the ventilator pushing air into the young man's lungs.

After the brief wake-up in the morgue, Steve had fallen unconscious; doctors and nurses had rushed him upstairs to the ICU, where he was now being kept under constant observation.

For five days, Tammy sat by his side wordlessly. She had not moved an inch; she told her mom that she was going to stay there until he got better, and she knew better than to argue. Once the adolescent made up her mind, there was no changing it whatsoever. Most of her relatives called her a "stubborn lil' cuss"; that fit her personality perfectly.

Tammy looked at her friend worriedly. The burns were very real; open, oozing wounds that leaked out a noxious reddish liquid that smelled like death. Others were charred over, leathery and blackish.

And then there were the hundreds of scars across his entire body. It appeared as if his veins and capillaries had burst all at once and rose to the surface, tattooing his skin freakishly.

Beep!
Beep!
Beep!

The noise was hypnotic; she felt lulled into a stupor as the—

"Tammy, any change?" Susan Haverton's voice broke through the trance, and the young lady almost shrieked.

"Nope. Nothing." She looked up at Steve's mom. "Where's Mr. Haverton?"

"Working. Where else? He don't give a damn about Steve." This was said with a fair amount of certainty, and for a moment, Tammy felt a tug on her heart. Poor Steve.

"Well, I'm not leaving until he wakes up. I owe him that much."

For one of the few times in her life, Susan smiled. "He's lucky to have a friend like you."

"Me, too."

A noise emanated from the bed. *"Urguhum!"*

Steve's now-bald head tossed back and forth on the pillow; it looked like he was in the throes of a bad dream.

"Urg! Ack!!" The noise was more urgent this time.

Suddenly, the lights dimmed in the ICU room and the monitor and ventilator powered off. A low, throbbing noise pulsated for a few moments around the young man, along with an eerie faint bluish light; then both ceased. At that exact moment, all the equipment popped back on and the lights returned to full brightness.

That looked just like the color of the lightning that hit Steve, Tammy thought eerily.

"Must be some lingering problems from the storms that moved through," Susan surmised. "That front did a lot of damage all over the place. Especially up in Missouri; those poor people. All those lives lost. What was the name of that town that was wiped out? Oh, yeah…Havendale. Wow. Those poor people," she repeated.

Steve's eyes snapped open. They were blood red, hemorrhaged from the strike. He clawed furtively at his vent tubing, finally snatching it out and throwing it to the floor. His IV went the same course. Then he bent over the bed, gagging. A thick, bluish mucus splattered onto the floor, and Tammy felt like heaving herself.

Bells and alarms began to go off. Nurses and doctors flooded the room and hovered over him.

A whisper; then, louder: "I'm fine. Give me some space."

A hand reached out to Tammy, and she took it gently. Steve looked deep into her eyes, then exhaled with gladness. "Hey there."

The young lady broke into tears. "Hey," she said, her voice breaking.

"I'm okay, Tam. No worries."

"No worries? You were *DEAD*, Steve! I saw your body in the morgue!"

Steve smiled through the pain. "Well, maybe I was…but not now."

"How're ya feeling?"

"Like a freakin' truck hit me, that's what," he explained with a croak. "And backed up and ran over me again." A slight chuckle escaped him.

His doctor, Pete Michaels, patted him gently on the arm as he took his vitals. "Okay, Steven, time to get some more rest." He held up a syringe. "Going to give you something more for your pain. I know those burns are hurting you pretty badly."

"Actually, Doc, not feeling anything right now. Thankfully."

Michaels looked concerned. "I am hoping that the lightning strikes didn't mess with your nerve endings too much, but there is that possibility," he admitted, then added, "best thing we can do right now is to keep you as pain-free as we can and let you heal. I've talked to your parents about sending you immediately to our burn center at Integris Health; they're one of the best in the nation."

Susan spoke up. "Doctor, I know that it's a high cost, but I've spoken to Medicaid, and they're gonna cover any expenses to help Steven get better."

Smiling, Michaels looked back down to his charge. "You'll be in good hands, Steven. They will do whatever it takes to get you well. I won't lie to you; it's going to be a long process. There'll be lots of days with pain; relearning some things damaged by the strike...but you'll get there, I promise. We can go ahead and arrange transport as soon as possible."

The young man shook his head. "I'm not going, doc. Just wanna go home and crash."

Everyone gave him a puzzled glance, Tammy included. "I would recommend against that, Steven. You still have a lot of healing to do," Dr. Michaels explained.

Steve shook his head a bit more forcefully. "Like I said, doc. I'm not going."

Tammy was dimly aware of the low hum starting again as the lights flickered brighter, eerily coinciding with Steve's growing anger. His mom and the doctor were fixated on the young man and didn't notice. The hum pitched higher and higher.

Whump! Whump!

Screams from outside the door as lights and ballasts exploded with fiery blue sparks, chasing employees, guests, and patients alike down the hallway. Alarms blared as people made for the exits.

Both adults stared in horror at Steve as he sat up in bed, ripped the IVs out of his arms, and walked unsteadily to the door. He turned around and gave them a cold stare. "I'm going home," he stated flatly, a cold blue gleam in his eyes.

And left.

Ray Campbell showed up a few days later.

Well, at least what was left of him.

The lifeless body was found tucked behind a grove of trees right next to the Seventh Day Adventist Church, not far from the Vicksburg Village apartments. It appeared that everything had been drained from the body until only a husk remained. His eye sockets and mouth stared wordlessly out of burnt-out sockets, affixed in a horrified eternal gaze. The police presence around the low-income housing units was relentless.

And as the cops mulled things over, Steve sat on his bed with his eyes closed, turning his hands over and over.

Tiny balls of blue lights moved over his fingers as he felt bits of energy course through him; trails of electricity trickled from the wall outlets and drifted towards him. As he stretched out his hands, blue beams rippled and surged into his fingers.

"Man, that feels...*fan-freakin'-tastic*."

As he continued to absorb the energy around him, the 8mm movie in his head unspooled the events of this past week.

Ray had finally confronted him a few blocks from his house one late evening, long after his parents had gone to bed amidst the chaos that had ensued after his short hospital stay. Doors were slammed, curse words were heard, and an overall mess was made.

Steve was sitting on the grass in back of the church, cooling his body temperature off. He had noticed, very strangely, that his body was running about three degrees above normal since the accident. Even ibuprofen didn't lower the fever, but it really didn't bother him in the least. He felt better with each passing day.

"Hey, it's lard ass!" Ray greeted him happily, and Steve scowled.

"Ain't got time for you, jerk face," he whispered back.

Ray feigned a pained look. "Jerk face?" He danced a little jig as the possibilities unfurled in his head about the upcoming beatdown on this punk. "Dude, you can do better than that. I'm fixin' to bring the pain, and all ya got is jerk face?"

Steve slowly stood up. "I got more for you than that," he explained and stretched out his hands, palms up.

An icy blue glow emanated from them. Ray stood, transfixed by the luminosity. It almost seemed… *alive*, pulsating in and out; in and out. The brightness gained in intensity.

And then, suddenly, beams of light shot out from Steve's fingers and slammed into Ray's body. He didn't have any time to scream as the glare engulfed him, then surged back to Steve, who soaked every single bit of it up gratefully.

Moments later, the smoking body of Ray Campbell collapsed to the ground, his light permanently extinguished.

Steve opened his eyes as the scene faded from his mind; his optics throbbed with that same bluish-white light.

And he smiled.

There was so much more energy to be had, and time was a-wastin'.

… AFTER MIDNIGHT

JEZEBEL

Richard E. Davis

AFTER MIDNIGHT

"And as if had been a light thing for him to walk in the sins of Jeroboam son of Nebat, he took as his wife Jezebel daughter of King Ethbaal of the Sidonians, and went and served Baal, and worshipped him."

1 Kings 16:31, ESV

Richard E. Davis

AFTER MIDNIGHT

A mob of people taunting her. Shouting, cursing. Falling. A sudden thud as her body hit the ground. The crushing weight of many feet.
Red-hot, bone-crunching pain as teeth gnawed into her.

Darkness.
Eons of black, silent nothingness.

Then, she found herself drifting above the landscape, the prevailing winds carrying her to and fro, up and down.

Mountains and lakes came into view; cities swept by, bustling with energy and activity. After a long time, she looked down through her ethereal presence at gigantic towers (*Babel?* her mind thought fleetingly) rising above the earth, and the throngs of people milling about below, like worker ants on assignment.

Up ahead in the twilight, a sign beckoned. Neon and glittering lights. An eight-pointed red star twinkling gaily. And the words swimming slowly into focus:

Welcome to Fabulous Las Vegas, Nevada.

Jezebel, once the mighty queen of Israel, wife of King Ahab, and scorned blasphemer of the Hebrew God Yahweh, sensed the wicked, sinful nature of thousands of souls permeating from all corners of this mighty golden city…and smiled wickedly.

She was back!

And this place created by man would be a nice place to start her earthly reign over again.

Benjamin "Ace" Tucker, explorer and ghost hunter extraordinaire, stepped out of his luxury limo and stretched.

With curly blonde shoulder-length locks and muscles to boot, Ace was the archetypical tv star. He regularly pulled in a "plus four" rating with around seven million weekly viewers, and he was being hailed as the "next big thing" in reality programming as his team chased poltergeists/spirits/ghosts/you name it all over the world.

"Spirit Snatchers" had made him a bonafide star.

Immediately, Ace was inundated by the paparazzi and signature seekers at the Luxor hotel, all of whom he welcomed with open arms and pen at the ready.

"Would you look at that?" his tech geek and go-to guy, Grant Hopkins, exclaimed. 'They flock to him like Yogi Bear to a picnic basket. Friggin' incredible."

Grant's periodic girlfriend, Megan, shook her head as she exited the geeked-out tech wagon. "Yeah, he thinks he's a rock star," she replied with a laugh.

"Always ready for another lay, but never a full-time stay."

A snort from the back, and then their intern April Forest emerged, frazzled by the long flight from the University of Wisconsin. "Any bets on how long it'll be until his first conquest?"

"Now now, people," retired pastor Elisa Gordon admonished them gently. "Sometimes Ace thinks with the wrong head is all."

"Sometimes?" Grant was aghast. "More like, does he actually have one upstairs to think with?

All of them laughed as they unloaded the van and made their way to the front desk. Ace was already there after skirting by most of his well-wishers, and the young man was flustered.

"We had specifically booked a set of rooms on the twelfth floor for our trip," he was explaining to the manager on duty. "It wasn't a request…it's a necessity for us to do our production from that specific location. I cleared it with your senior management as well."

"And, of course, we here at The Luxor want to accommodate your requests, Mr. Tucker. I do apologize for the confusion. Please give me a few moments to see what I can do for you, sir." With that, the manager hurriedly walked off.

"Bunch of a-holes," Ace surmised, then took in the atrium view. "Quite impressive, if ya ask me."

"Built for $375 million by Circus Circus Enterprises," Grant ticked off with each finger. "Dozens of unexplained deaths, paranormal activity on numerous floors, replicas of ancient Egyptian structures which may be conducive to dark energy and forces…yeah, it's a regular roller coaster of fear."

"Except that the majority of each of those things can be explained away by science, not religion, and not from 'artificial science', Grant." Elisha stood with hands on hips, looking for an argument.

"You'll get no pushback from me, Eli," insisted Grant. "Just trying to make sense of it all."

Ace laughed, a crooked smile lighting up his face. "We're not here to make sense of anything, G. We're here to make some dough and bed the ho's!"

"Good God, man. Do you ever let up?" Megan was exasperated, and it showed in her demeanor. "Be serious! We've got work to do later."

Ace tipped a wink to them, and then began barking some orders to the concierge staff about their luggage.

The blinding light beckoned her, whispering and wanting.

It shot up from the pyramid into the night sky like a homing beacon, welcoming bugs, bats, and birds from miles around into its death-inducing heat and glare; once in the doomed orbit of the beam, nothing escaped.

Jezebel eyed the light with interest. She could sense…no, feel would be a better word; dozens of trapped souls within the boundaries of the building, desperate for release. Hoping for a reprieve from their bondage. Praying for a miracle that never came.

And she smiled. She could give them that, plus much more.

But first, they would have to do her bidding.

And then…*all* the world would bow down and worship her once again.

The team's bags were unpacked and equipment set up along the empty twelfth-floor hallway; all they were waiting for was the show's host.

Grant checked his watch for the umpteenth time. "Where in the hell is Ace?"

Megan chuckled. "Last I saw of him, he was grooming one of his 'most ardent' fans down in the lobby. They disappeared a few minutes later."

"I'll bet they just disappeared," April snorted. "He's prolly got her stashed away in his room right now."

"Got who stashed away where?" Ace called out from down the hallway. His hair was perfectly groomed and his complexion flawless.

"Your latest conquest is who," Grant joked.

Ace strode up to them, shaking his head. "My dear friend, my feelings are hurt. You must think me an incorrigible heathen." He stopped, then grinned. "And, by the way, her name is Heather, and she's a peach."

"I knew it," April concluded. "You just couldn't help yourself, could you?"

"But I did help myself, April. And I feel so much better, knowing that all of you are always looking out for me."

Grant waved his hands dismissively. "Okay, I just don't want to know, dude." He motioned towards the equipment. "Everything's set up, boss. Let's go ahead and do a few sound checks and then get the ball rolling."

Jezebel descended into the light.

There was momentary warmth. Then, darkness illuminated only by a door's outline. Jezebel floated down a long, dimly lit corridor until she came across two doors adorned with a large placard: 30.

Strange markings, she thought, a confused look on her ageless and pale face. Not Hebrew, Aramaic, or Egyptian…but something else…

A voice whispered.

English.

English? Oh, yes. The guttural and crude language of this territory, the inner muse informed her. She glanced at the symbols again. 30.

Numbers. Signifying…levels? No; floors would be the better term.

Jezebel smiled.

With each passing moment, her understanding of this world was made more manifest; unintelligible words became clear thoughts, and those concepts were coalescing into soon-to-be actions.

So as the otherworldly presence known as Jezebel explored, she absorbed the nefarious energy that was all around her.

In the Luxor.

And in this town called Sin City.

She felt rejuvenated; reborn; *renewed*.

And as Jezebel's power grew, it had other dire consequences for the world around her.

On the horizon, a storm front was brewing. Distant lightning flashed and thunder rumbled across the arid valleys below. Ominous rolling clouds violently churned in the twilight sky as the thunderstorm billowed its distinct anvil shape into the upper atmosphere. Sheets of rain began cascading onto the parched land as the storm progressed forward, inching closer and closer to its final destination.

Las Vegas, Nevada.

Grant heard the first sounds of thunder rolling towards them, even through the thick walls of the Luxor.

And inexplicably, the hair on his arms rose as goosebumps ran down his back. He shivered uncontrollably.

"You okay, bud?" Ace has a questioning look on his face.

Grant nodded slightly. "Yeah, man. Just a sudden chill." He glanced up and down the vacant hallways; Ace had reserved the entire floor just for their party, so they could film the upcoming episode with no interruptions. It was deathly and eerily quiet, the dim lights providing an even more foreboding overlay to the scene.

April noticed the overbearing sense of dread as well. "Yeah, me too," she admitted. "Felt this before at some of our other projects but not as strongly. I don't particularly believe in what we do, but this…" She trailed off, and Grant knew exactly how she felt.

Ace was practically giddy. "That's what I want to hear, team! Ain't nothing like a good haunt to scare the piss out of our beloved tv audience!" He laughed. "Ratings galore!!"

Grant hoisted one of the cams up to his shoulder. "Let's get this thing going, boss. Sooner we get done, the better."

Elisha, the eternal debunker, gave a small laugh. "You guys are something else," he admonished. "Low lights and a few chills and you wanna tuck tail and run."

April grinned despite her fear. "I believe in flight before fight, Elisha. It's kept me safe so far."

At that moment, thunder rattled the windows as a lightning bolt sizzled across the peak of the Luxor. The lights briefly flickered.

"That one was pretty close," Megan whispered.

Another flash, then *BANG!* The hall bulbs dimmed, brightened, then popped off. Groans and wailing could be faintly heard from the lobby over a hundred feet below as the entire structure was plunged into darkness. A few moments later, emergency lights slowly came on and feebly illuminated the scene.

"Well, this puts a damper on things," Ace surmised, which prophetically would turn out to be quite true.

Outside, hail and rain pounded down on the city as the lightning continued unabated. Multiple strikes hit The Strat and shattered windows along the observation deck, sending shards of death to the hapless below. The Palazzo, Waldorf Astoria, and Fountainbleau also took direct beatings from the weather. People ran screaming in all directions, trying to seek refuge in buildings; under awnings; anywhere to get a brief respite.

The chaos was widespread and devastating.

And this was only the beginning of Jezebel's fury.

Ace was now in his element.

They had set up battery-powered floodlights to help combat the gloom. Unlike the rest of the building, the twelfth floor was cozily lit and warm.

"Las Vegas…the city of intrigue, and legend," he began, with a serious inflection to his voice. "And one building, in particular, stands out when speaking of things both mysterious and eerie." Ace walked to the banister that overlooked the structure's atrium and stretched out his arms. "This is the Luxor, where paranormal activity runs rampant. This is tonight's focus on Spirit Snatchers." He paused for a moment, then smiled. "And….cut! Perfect take, everyone!"

Grant nodded from behind the camera. "Nice intro." He gestured over to April. "Hey April, let's get things set up for the next shot. We can pick it up at the banister and then have the drone do a high-def shot from the atrium looking back at Ace."

"I'll get the mini setup ready," April concurred.

Megan turned to their teammate and former pastor with a concerned look on her face. "What do you know about The Luxor, Elisha?"

"Just the usual. Multiple deaths were supposedly covered up by the contractors and local government. Lots of alleged ghost sightings when they opened up the Titanic exhibit. The blonde haunting this floor. And the list goes on and on." He shrugged as a long roll of thunder rumbled the building. "If people look hard enough, they will always find something that is not easily explained."

"And what do you think of those types of things?"

Elisha paused while he collected his thoughts, then spoke slowly. "Megan, I truly believe that there are things in this world that can't be explained away by science or religion. We try our best to understand them and still come up short." He looked at Ace, then shook his head. "And instead of trying to come up with explanations, maybe we should just let them be and move on. After all, we do our best to play God and figure things out on our own…and that doesn't work out very well most of the time."

The young lady looked at Elisha curiously. "That sounds weird, coming from a former pastor."

Elisha smiled. "What you just heard is my position…not from a religious viewpoint, nor a scientific one. Just my own humble opinions on the matter."

Ace ventured over. "Okay, El, I couldn't help but hear your thoughts. What do you think about what I am doing with the show? Seriously?"

"Glad you asked," Elisha remarked. "What I think you're doing is utter nonsense and total bullshit."

Ace was taken aback. "Say what?"

"Just my humble opinion, Ace. You asked, and I delivered."

"Well, then," Ace began, "I think that—"

A blood-curdling scream from down below stopped them all dead in their tracks.

The spirit of Jezebel had arrived.

She flew with singular purpose around the main lobby of the Luxor, and with each pass, grew stronger and more visible as she sucked in the life force of each sinful soul. Her flowing and fragile robes were now blood-stained, tattered, and dirty cloths, reeking of decay and wretchedness. Her ungodly laughter cut through the ear-piercing shrieks and wails of the dying as they lay convulsing on the tiled floor, their faces sunken in, drained of all humanness.

There is soooo much depravity here, she greedily thought. *More than enough.*

She lifted her head and primally screamed into the heavens. And as she was doing so, she caught a glimpse of bright lights far above her.

"My God," Elisha breathed as he watched the carnage unfold. "What is that thing floating around?"

Ace was dumbfounded. "What in the hell is going on?"

Grant tugged at both of their sleeves. "Gents, we need to go somewhere ASAP. Whatever's going on, it doesn't look good."

They all took off in a run, headed down the hall to Ace's room.

Once inside, with the door secured, Ace turned to Elisha worriedly. "What in the hell were we just seeing, man?"

Elisha looked at him with an unsettled gaze. "I don't know, Ace. It appeared to be…some kind of corporeal spirit."

"English, El!"

"For lack of a better term, a physical spirit manifestation of some sort." Elisha paused to take in a deep breath. "And it looked like it was sucking the life out of people."

"What? Sucking the life out of people?"

The ex-minister nodded, his Adam's apple bobbing as he swallowed deeply. "You heard me."

Megan was petrified. "Wuh…where did it come from?"

"No clue. It showed up right after the power went out."

As if on cue, a huge arcing bolt slammed into the Luxor and lit up the night sky. A second later, *CRACK!* as the accompanying thunder split the sky.

"God Almighty," Elisha breathed. "I felt the hair on my arms standing up just then."

"Me too," Grant agreed. He glanced at his cell phone.

No service.

"Just freakin' great," he surmised. "Can't even call emergency services. This just sucks on so many —"

A light tapping on the door.

All of them stood, frozen in place, as the tapping continued. Then, a woman's voice, small and pleading, in an unknown language.

שלום? מישהו שם?

"What is that?" Ace questioned in a whisper.

Elisha leaned into the door. The voice called out again.

"Oh my God…it's ancient Hebrew," he translated. "Asking if there's anyone here. But why would she be —"

Suddenly, the door burst apart, and a hand reached in and through Elisha's chest, then pulled back to reveal the young man's still-beating heart, dripping with blood. He stood there for a few moments, transfixed at the sight, and then collapsed.

Jezebel floated into the room, her eyes blazing with red-hot hatred. She held out the gory organ for all to see, then expanded her mouth around it and swallowed it whole.

Megan screamed. So did the others.

Jezebel smiled; a long, slow grin that told of horrors yet to come.

Later, after the decimation of the ghost-hunting team and all those in the Luxor, she levitated above the hotel and basked in the constant lightning bolts that illuminated her glory.

Her first conquest was complete.

And there was much; yes, *much* more to come.

REVENGE OF THE KILLER HAY BALES

Richard E. Davis

The news headlines were vicious and unrelenting:

"Man Torches Town Over Unrequited Love!" screamed the National Enquirer; USA Today was milder, but still fierce with propaganda: *"Disaster at Clear Lake, Georgia: Why Did He Do It?"* Hundreds more chimed in with Internet blogs/vlogs, podcasts, and viral social media...but yet, no one knew the *true* story.

And that, my dear friends, is the age-old saga of revenge.

The evidence of mass slaughter was burnt out of existence with the destruction of Clear Lake five years ago; no one left to tell the tale of the twisted "awakening" that the hay bales experienced on that fateful day...and no one left to explain the sickening wreckage of crushed cars and people along the highway leading into the burned-out town.

A mystery, indeed.

Fortunately, the casualties were less than two hundred, and the scars upon the land quickly healed. Clear Lake, Georgia was never rebuilt, and a small memorial marker stood as a powerful and mute reminder near the former downtown area. And, as always, life went on, and the disaster was soon forgotten.

Forgotten to humans, that is…but to the bale population, it was a folk story that was passed along from farm to farm, from generation to generation. A redemption tale of survival, revenge, and happy endings.

A tale that, unfortunately, would be repeated two years later and over a thousand miles away.

Missouri was called the Show-Me state for many reasons; perhaps the most widely known statement came from U.S. Congressman Willard Duncan Vandiver during a speech in Philadelphia in 1899. In it, he coined this famous phrase: "I come from a state that raises corn and cotton and cockleburs and Democrats, and frothy eloquence neither convinces nor satisfies me. I am from Missouri. You have got to show me."

Wise words from a politician, except when dealing with hay bales.

Known for its abundant corn and soybean crops, Missouri was also home to thousands of cattle, primarily raised for beef consumption. And with cows came a natural by-product: the aforementioned freshly rolled hay for their food.

On this fateful day, just as before, the hay achieved its "consciousness" again; a state that was neither slumbering, nor awake, but somewhere in between; an almost surreal extension of existence. A place where the only thing on their collective minds was that thick and dark substance that oozed from the human body known as *blood*.

So, as they waited, silent and watchful, alongside these Midwestern fence rows; in fields, and under the cover of plastic moisture barriers, they rocked; they murmured, and they sang a quiet song.

A little ditty called revenge...*oh how sweet*.

And those in the Show-Me State were going to be shown what clobbering time was all about.

Camp Derry was a mean lean city of 1,200 along U.S. Highway 136 and County Road YY; its only claim to fame was proximity to the booming micropolis of Havendale, located just six miles to the west. Almost seventy-five percent of the population commuted to their employment at the Nodaway County Hydroponics Corporation; good wages, fairly easy work, and a generous benefits package.

On this scorching and humid July 3rd, most of the town was peacefully quiet before the annual big kickoff to summer: Camp Derry's Independence Day Fest, a weekend complete with the requisite carnival, fireworks, pie-eating contests, free concerts, and awesome food. City trucks were busy with last-minute preparations like banner hanging and flower watering; carnies scampered around like ants evicted from their home, ready for the sun to drop and their nightly ritual to begin.

All in all, just another small-town, fun-filled holiday weekend.

But there would be a twist in the day's plan.

A deadly twist.

Theodore Hannity, self-proclaimed best local pot farmer around, trampled through the thick underbrush around the back of his 500-acre property, swinging a machete right and left while cursing under his breath. He had let his "pot trail" grow over these past few weeks, and he was finding the way to his latest planting quite difficult.

So here he was, painstakingly retracing his footsteps with a goofy grin on his face. It didn't help that he was currently half-stoned on some nice red-haired sinsemilla bud from last year's crop. The smoke kept some of the B-52 bomber mosquitoes from sucking most of his body's blood. They drifted alongside Hannity like a real-life montage of Joe Cartoon's "Stoned Flies".

"Thank God for the small stuff," he mused.

Five minutes later, he broke free into a small clearing, devoid of weeds but with some nice overhanging limbs. Those helped to protect his crop from those pesky county planes which flew overhead several times per week, desperately trying to find his prized marijuana crops. Hannity was a street-smart stoner; he kept his plants scattered among numerous locations around his property and adjacent lands (much to the chagrin of his neighbors). That way, he could still make a decent profit while denying any knowledge of "someone else" planting on his turf.

"Man, plants are lookin' nice," he observed as his smile drew even wider. "This Super Miracle-Gro is the BOMB!"

Plenty of moisture and abundant sunshine were adding up to a bumper crop for Hannity this year. Ten plants were in this location, and all of them were over five feet tall with deep green leaves and buds protruding everywhere. The sweet smell of mary jane hung over the still-humid July air.

"Woohoo! I'm in the money, I'm in the money, so..."

Hannity's voice trailed off as he gazed off into the distance; there, about 400 yards away, was a sight that (high or not) would make a grown man wet all over himself.

With all the stealth of a band of ninjas, a small group of freshly banded hay bales slowly rolled through the tall grass and weeds. The only noise was an eerie swish swish swish as they inched their way forward, oblivious to everything...even Hannity. They seemed to have an odd, determined focus; at least, that's what the man's foggy, pot-deluded brain told him.

"Think it's about time to step away from the party, dude," he whispered, and carefully backed up. Five feet; ten feet...and at fifteen feet, he stepped right into a woodchuck hole. There was a sickening twist, then *snap!* and Hannity howled out in agony. Nesting birds in the surrounding trees took flight immediately, rudely chirping displeasure at being disturbed from their mid-day naps.

The bales stopped; then ever-so-slowly turned to face the hapless young man. He shrieked and yanked his useless foot out of the hole; it flopped crazily and with each movement excruciating pain shot up his leg.

He sat down hard, tears streaming down his face. In that instant, he remembered reading about Clear Lake; the headlines; the burning hay; hell, he remembered *everything*.

And, after a mute and deadly serious stare down, the hay rocked forward...then backward...and then...

AFTER MIDNIGHT

Rolled towards him.
 The last thought that crossed Theodore Hannity's mind was...*my God, what did I ever do to them any--*
 Once the brief carnage was complete, the bales moved on.

Flashes of intense light:
blueredgreen.
Then darkness.

Another memory: brief scenes of a time almost forgotten--
screamingpeoplebloodfirepain.
 A macabre sense of a job well done and accomplished; the sort of feeling one would get after pushing their chair back with belly painfully full and buttons stretched out to their limits.

whatisgoalwhatisgoalwhatisgoal

This continuous thought ran through the mass consciousness of the bales; their previous challenge had been met, but at a terrible cost to the populace. They had been fragmented; broken; scattered to farms/fields/or fed once again to their dreaded nemesis, Cow

Land. Only now were they beginning to piece together their history and the ultimate destiny awaiting.

Weakly at first, and then with increasing intensity, the lead bale put out one message. As it passed from one to another the voice grew and swelled; then trumpeted throughout the entire bale nation.

One chilling and endless phrase:

destroykilldestroykilldestroykilldestroykilldestroyk illdestroykill

And with that, the bales understood.

The time was very near at hand.

Mayor Stu Dalton surveyed his "kingdom" from the steps of Camp Derry's City Hall/Police Dept./Courthouse and saw that it all was good.

Very good.

Everything was in place and ready for the festivities, and there was still time to spare. Time to bask in the glory of another successful start to summer in northwestern Missouri, and watch the money roll into the town's coffers.

In his fifth year (and newly re-elected) to the mayoral position, Dalton was sitting pretty in the driver's seat. What made things even better: he wasn't an original settler to the town; in fact, he was a Havendale native. His brother Ted was a long-tenured sciences instructor at Havendale Sr. High, and was one of the few survivors from the devastating tornadic outbreak in April 2025.

The surrounding area had seen its share of devastation, but as the saying goes, hope springs eternal. From the ashes, beauty did indeed rise. Havendale was rebuilt better than ever, and more people were moving into the area to enjoy great jobs and some excellent weather. Camp Derry was growing, small businesses were moving in, and life was good.

Dalton smiled broadly and inwardly mused, *"If only the naysayers could see me now...no one ever thought I would amount to anything."*

With a renewed skip in his step, he dismounted his perch and gladly joined the ever-growing crowd that was gathering downtown.

It was turning out to be a very good day.

Just as the people were massing into bigger numbers, so, too, were the bales as they crept closer and closer to Camp Derry.

From expansive farms they rolled; from the "field nurseries" they came, tiny rectangular bales carried on the backs of their surrogate cousins; from barns they exploded into sight, ecstatic to breathe in the fresh air and feel the sunlight on their grassy backs.

Tens turned into hundreds which gave way to thousands. And yet, for their massive populace, they were strangely silent as they traversed the land. The bales had learned a valuable lesson from their trial run...

And *stealth* would be the killing order for this day.

The distance slowly ticked down; five, then three; and now just two scant miles separated the bales from their goal.

No dust cloud...no thunderous rumbling would herald their presence as before; instead, the ambush would be like one gigantic, nauseous fart that stings the eyes and leaves one gasping for air.

Silent...but deadly.

Tommy Parker, Nodaway County Sheriff, was out cruising the highways and byways of his territory, gearing himself up for what was going to amount to a raucous, beer-filled and fueled weekend.

"Yup, gonna be one for the record books," he muttered to the weeds whizzing by the open window. "Wonder how many we can fill the cells with?"

He was still chuckling as he rolled up to Ted Hannity's house, ready to serve the warrant at hand.

AFTER MIDNIGHT

This one, as the many numerous ones before it, was for the cultivation and possession of more than ten cannabis plants; the newly-passed state law allowed for personal recreational use only, and Hannity tended to abuse it to line his pockets with cash. His loose interpretation was a constant thorn for Sheriff Parker, but it did result in hefty fines and some jail time for this pot-loving loser.

As Parker exited his vehicle, one immediate thought struck him: it was quiet.

Too quiet.

No blaring music; no loud and raucous crowd.

Nothing.

At this time of day, Hannity usually had the party starting to crank up with his dopehead friends wandering around in and around his property. They pretty much kept to themselves and didn't cause much of a scene, and the young man lived far enough away from his neighbors that the cops weren't called out too often.

So, this was rather puzzling to Parker. Where was everyone?

"Hannity? Ted Hannity?" the lawman called out into the stillness. "You there, bud?" He tried knocking on the wide-open front door. "Anyone home?"

With a slow patient motion guided by years of experience, Parker loosened the strap from his state-issued Glock pistol and kept a wary hand on the grip as he stepped into the house.

Beer bottles and paper plates were scattered everywhere; the reek of mold and alcohol permeated every inch of the living space. Sheriff Parker quickly glanced around, and seeing no one in sight, proceeded through the trash-filled kitchen, bedrooms, and out the back door. No one was there, either.

Then he remembered the small dirt trail that led into the "grow fields", as Hannity so eloquently called them. With that in mind, the sheriff cautiously made the trek down to a grisly discovery.

"Oh my word," Parker muttered under his breath. "What in the blue blazes happened here?"

Dark splotches painted onto a grisly canvas of weeds and grass (*so much blood*, his mind whispered); that was the horrific view that lay before this veteran lawman.

Hannity's life liquid was spilled over a fifteen to twenty-foot area, and lying smashed beyond recognition before him was (undoubtedly) the mutilated, flattened remains of the former pot-smoking rebel.

His gorge rose quickly into his throat, and he promptly upchucked what was left of this morning's breakfast. After a few moments, the heaving subsided to some dry retching, and Parker shakily wiped a hand across his mouth.

"My God...I've gotta get someone out here quick," he realized out loud.

And that was the one thing he said that he would regret for the rest of his very short life.

A dull roar suddenly filled the air, gaining in pitch and volume as the seconds passed by. Parker wheeled around and was rudely confronted by fifteen large and slightly ticked-off hay bales bearing down on his location.

With a slightly womanish scream, he ran down the path and into the supposedly "safe" confines of the recently deceased Hannity's home. However, the bales did not care whether he was inside; outside; in the air; or up a creek without a paddle.

The latter of which the sheriff was now facing.

And the water was *VERY* deep.

Parker's last vision was of the bale herd exploding into the house, demolishing walls, windows, and this hapless human who happened to be in the wrong place, at the wrong time.

And John McClane from Die Hard he was not.

Once the carnage was over, the bales moved on.

Homage to Clear Lake, part 1.
thetimehascomethetimehascomethetimehascome
The bale nation gradually rolled to a stop.

Their leader, One, edged out from the rest and turned to face her compatriots. In those wordless moments, information was exchanged; ideas were transferred; and the plan was digested and understood. It would not take long. Their revenge would be precise and transformational. Humankind would finally glimpse the main course after the appetizer that was served at Clear Lake.

Twenty-two thousand, six hundred and fifty bales began to oscillate towards Camp Derry in a purposefully direct manner. A high, almost musical tone followed them; it was almost like the bales were…

Singing.

It was killin' time at last.

Homage to Clear Lake, part 2.
Death and destruction were laid bare. There was nothing and no one left. Just flames, wreckage, and endless blood and gore.

The fires kept burning…

AFTER MIDNIGHT

And the bales continued rolling...
For miles.

The final war had just begun.

Richard E. Davis

CHAIN LIGHTNIN' (Part Two)

Richard E. Davis

AFTER MIDNIGHT

Noun: lightning that appears to move very rapidly in a long, angular, zigzag, or forked course.
Merriam Webster Dictionary

Richard E. Davis

> *Scurry*: Meaning that implies "to move very rapidly
> in a hurry, making a rush, or forced course."
>
> — Merriam-Webster Dictionary

Steve Haverton was on the lam.

Now the cops were looking for him; their excuse was to "question" him concerning the suspicious circumstances surrounding Ray Campbell's death.

Steve knew better. They were going to pin it on him, no matter how hard he would try to explain, persuade, or play the hapless victim.

The young man had left his home a few weeks back and made a quick beeline to the tall woods surrounding Lake Thunderbird State Park. Even though the trek was a long ten miles, the trees provided him cover, and for whatever reason, they also comforted him. He could not only feel the energy they gave off but could also "see" it in wavy patterns that floated through the stillness surrounding him.

And, the vacant seasonal homes dotting the lake gave him ample food and water. His newfound ability was handy in breaking in without leaving behind any clues. It was as simple as manipulating the energy surrounding the deadbolt, then slowly opening it.

Easy peasy lemon squeezy.

Of course, after each use, he would have to "recharge" his batteries. Little things like locks didn't take much; others, like zapping the lake's waters so he could catch fish to eat took a ton out of him. Thankfully, there was plenty of wildlife around to harness energy from. He just had to be careful to not draw attention to himself when he trekked out of the woods for supplies.

So…he kept busy.

At the very forefront of his mind was keeping a list and checking it twice (Santa wasn't the only one to have nice and naughty categories), and making sure that whoever crossed him in the future would pay for it dearly.

His parents were the prime example.

On the evening he left, his dad exploded, smacking him all over the house while his mom cowered back, afraid to say anything. Steve took the first three or four blows, but then, as his anger built to a crescendo…well, then it became clobberin' time.

And boy, did he ever put the hammer down. In the span of about three point two seconds, there was nothing left but a withered, burnt-out shell where his father once stood; the corpse's expression spoke volumes: an open-mouthed, *"oh crap"* moment frozen in high-definition, three-dimensional glory for the whole world to see.

Of course, then his mom started screaming, so he had to tie up that loose end. When all was said and done, his energy needs were satisfied, but he had to make like a tree and leave the decedents behind.

The woods beckoned to him, and Steve heeded the call.

Tammy was worried about her friend.

For days on end, the police had stopped by their apartment, looking for Steve. Drilling her on when she saw him last; had she talked to him at all; if she knew of any hiding places where he might be; etc. etc. etc. And repeatedly, she had nothing to tell them. After a while, they mercifully left her alone.

Except for the nondescript dark blue car that was stationed across the street, pointing towards the apartment complex, with a lone occupant seated.

"Bastards," she muttered under her breath. "Why can't they just leave me alone?"

Stu Sullivan was also worried about his former student.

He took a keen interest in the young man since he had seen a few viral videos of Steve juggling tennis balls in mid-air, and the blue "mist" that surrounded him. It appeared that these short clips were taken from a hidden vantage point and then zoomed in to see the action.

"My God…they're not even touching his hands. How?"

Being the science nerd he was, Stu dove into the books and found out everything he could about electrokinesis: in superhero lore, it was the ability to psychically generate and manipulate electrical fields and/or energy.

Yeah, yeah, Stu thought aimlessly. Just a bunch of horse hockey. *No way that someone could get hit by lightning and survive…much less have those kinds of powers. Something else has to be going on with Steve. But what? And where is he?*

With that, he wandered out onto his back deck and gazed at the far shoreline of Lake Thunderbird; he could see the glow of Norman's city skyline just above the tree line. He loved living just far enough away to enjoy some of the creature comforts of country living while being close enough to civilization to hop in his car and make the 10-15 minute jaunt into town. It was a blessing and one that he—

Bursts of bluish light shot up into the sky from the woods just across the lake as a distant dying scream punctuated the darkness. Two; five; then two more flashes in quick succession.

Then silence.

"What the hell?" Stu whispered, his eyes still locked on the woods.

Nothing replied to him. And foolishly, he scooped up his key to the ATV and headed to the garage. It wouldn't take him long to pop over to the west side of the lake, check things out, and get back in time for Monday Night Football.

Or maybe that was just wishful thinking on his part.

Steve stood over the lifeless mountain lion, breathing heavily.

Boy, that took a lot out of me, he thought. Steve had to hit that sucker nine times before it decided to give up the ghost. It usually only took two good hits and people were goners.

"I tip my hat to you, good creature," he snorted and gave an exaggerated bow. "You put up one helluva fight."

The "blue mist of death" (that's what he called it, for no other reason other than it sounded cool) gently rose from the lion's carcass, and Steve reached out his hands to it. Delicate tendrils of electricity spiraled out and crept into him, and he shuddered in delight. Every time he recharged, he felt...*new*.

But he also realized, with dread, that he was needing more and more to keep him satisfied.

He heard an engine revving through the woods, coming closer and closer to his location. He turned his palms up and looked at them; the blue was still very faint.

"Not enough," he muttered, and his gaze shifted to the bright ATV lights.

"But *that* should be more than enough."

And Steve grinned.

Taking no chances, Stu dialed 911 while on the way to his destination and informed the dispatcher of his suspicions about what the blue lights could be.

"You need to send some officers out this way, pronto," he explained. "If this turns out to be Steve, he looks to be armed and very dangerous." Of course, he left out the part of what exactly the young man was armed with; that would be another conversation to be had when they got there.

The teacher reached the far woods and shut the engine off. The slow tick-tick-tick of it cooling off was the lone sound he heard as he dismounted the off-road vehicle, and for a fleeting moment, he wondered where all the other animals were and why he didn't hear them when—

WHOOMP! A flash of intense blue light hit the ATV and it exploded, sending a tremendous ball of fire into the sky and throwing Stu into the shallow end of the lake. He came up, sputtering.

"Holy Mother of God," he mumbled and shook himself off. The dampness of the night air made him shiver.

"Oh, crap, Mr. Sullivan! I'm sorry! Didn't know it was you." Steve stepped out of the shadows and into the crackling light of the ruined vehicle.

"Steve?"

"Yes, sir. I've been living in the woods for a few weeks now. Thought it best to get out of town before the stuff hit the fan."

Stu shook his head. "The police have been searching for you, son," his instructor explained. "There's a lot of people worried about you and wanting to ask you what happened to your parents."

Steve chuckled. "They know what happened to them, Mr. Sullivan; all they want to do is hunt me down and put me away."

"Steve, I can help you," Stu offered. "You can come back to my house and we can sort things out."

The youth shook his head. "I'm not going back. Ever." There were tears in his eyes, and he brushed them away indifferently. "I'm a freak with powers. I killed Ray. Then my dad. And mom. They got in my way."

Stu felt his fear welling up inside of him but shoved it down. "Got in your way? My God, why?"

They were interrupted by rustling in the woods, and then four armed policemen lifted their flashlights, guns pointed directly at him. "Steve Haverton!" one of them yelled. "Put your hands up and kneel! You're under arrest for the murders of James and Susan Haverton and Ray Campbell!! Do it now!"

Steve turned to his teacher with a faint smile on his face; the tears were flowing rapidly now. "Can you do me a favor, Mr. Sullivan? Can you tell Tammy thanks for being such a great friend?" His lower lip started trembling. "I loved her and she was always there for me."

Steve swiveled back towards the law enforcement personnel as he raised his hands; not in surrender, but in opposition. Bluish energy began pouring out from his body.

"I'll say it one more time, Haverton. *GET ON THE GROUND NOW!!*"

Steve's eyes were now glowing white. He grinned, then pointed a finger at the nearest officer and blew his head off with a smoldering laser light. Bits of gray matter and skull fragments rained down on the gathering.

The cops began firing indiscriminately. Dozens of bullets plowed into the young man's body as he jerked and twitched like a hapless scarecrow. The blue light sizzled, dimmed, and then extinguished as his body finally hit the ground with a thud.

Stu's legs buckled; he knelt beside his student and shook his head. "Oh, Steve…why?" There were no more words. "Why?"

In the distance, a faint ambulance's siren wailed.

Later.

The morgue was eerily quiet; Steve's body lay motionless under a thick white sheet as the coroner and two plainclothes police officers stood outside the doors, conversing quietly.

"What a mess," one of the cops opined. "Sure didn't see that coming."

Officer #2 nodded in agreement. "Yeah. First, he offs his bully. Can't say I blamed him on that one; guy got what he deserved. But then his mom and dad? WTF?"

"He was a very disturbed young man," the coroner concurred. "Very disturbed for sure."

All three walked down the hallway in a slow shuffle. So many questions.

And so few answers.

Even later.
Inky blackness.
Then, faintly at first, a bluish hue was seen underneath the sheet. It swelled by the minute, becoming brighter and brighter until the glow dispelled all the darkness in the room.
Steve Haverton sat up, the sheet sliding off his now-healed body. He lifted his hands and watched the cold blue light arcing, then grinned devilishly.

PULPIT

Richard E. Davis

"That ain't nuthin' but a piece of old wood."
　　　　　　　　　　Steven Renfield

Richard E. Davis

The back door of True Light Ministries flung open, and a disheveled young man stumbled out into the bitter winter air in Cambridge Falls, Wisconsin.

Newly appointed pastor Rev. Kevin Spaulding breathed in once; twice; then leaned over the railing and promptly blew chunks everywhere. This was his third Sunday in the pulpit at this new assignment, and it showed badly.

Once the heaving subsided, he took inventory of himself.

The collar on: *Check*.

Hair ok? He ran his finger through his scalp and smoothed the 'do down. *Check*.

Get anything on your clothes? He did a cursory scan. Nothing there. *Check*.

Sermon notes: *Check*.

He turned around and headed back to the sanctuary, taking a moment to stop by the bathroom and do a quick rinse and spit with mouthwash.

The small congregation was patiently waiting on him as his wife continued to pound out "The Old Rugged Cross" on the piano while looking at him worriedly. Julie Ann had been a faithful spouse to Kevin; three years and a set of twins into their marriage, he informed her that he felt God was calling him into the ministry. At first, Julie was shocked, but after many long nights in prayer and discussions about their future, she packed the family up (including the twins, Thomas and Michelle) and they headed to Asbury University.

Four years and a Pastoral Ministries Program graduate later, Kevin embarked on his spiritual journey; ordination with WELS (the Wisconsin Evangelical Lutheran Synod) and first heading the flock at a small local faith community in Fox Lake, then a larger one in Fond du Lac. Now, he was finally tasked to build a struggling church in Cambridge Falls, just outside of Lost Lake near Beaver Dam.

And this was proving to be his biggest challenge yet. The people were welcoming, but somewhat resistant to the changes that the good reverend was hoping to bring to the local body of believers, which consisted of farmers and "old money" congregants. On any given Sunday, there were 30-40 regulars in attendance.

Kevin was frustrated at the closed minds of some of the people, and today's sermon was going to address that. How it went over, though, was yet to be seen.

"My good brothers and sisters in the Lord Jesus Christ," Kevin began. "I stand before you this morning with a heavy heart; it is burdened by the lack of our outreach to the local community. And I, for one, am willing to shoulder part of that blame. This servant needs to do better; be better; in how I interact with those who are the least, the last, and the lost."

Silence. A few puzzled glances among the congregants. He pressed on.

"For too long, this building has not been used for its main purpose: to be a lighthouse for the area, shining the light and hope of Christ for the world to see, and to draw those in who are in need of the saving grace that only our Lord and Savior can offer. Quite bluntly, we have become complacent in our mission, and the Lord is giving us a message this morning; that message is to do better. Do more. And most of all, to start *doing it now.*"

Some nods and murmurs of agreement, mostly from the younger folks. The money people sat with arms crossed, waiting to hear more. *And maybe even waiting to pounce.* Kevin smiled. God wasn't going to let them have their way as the young minister felt the presence of the Holy Spirit in the building.

It was time for them to really hear The Word.

"God requires our best, and not what we want to give him," he continued. "Second Timothy, chapter two, and verse fifteen tells us to 'do your best to present yourself to God as one approved; a worker who does not need to be ashamed, rightly handling the word of truth.' Proverbs says 'Commit your work to the Lord, and your plans will be established.' That's sixteen verse three. Colossians three verse seventeen: 'And whatever you do, in word and in deed, do everything in the name of the Lord Jesus, giving thanks to God the Father through Him'."

Kevin took a deep breath. *Well, here goes nothing*. "The Lord spoke to me last night while I was finalizing this message, and what He said shook me to the core. It was just a few words posed in the form of a question. And it was this: My son, we need to move forward as a Body in Christ. What will *you* do to make it happen?"

He stared at the congregation; he could tell that a few of them were *very* uncomfortable with the sermon. It showed in their demeanor; their scowls; their heads shaking back and forth in displeasure. And yet, the words kept coming out of his mouth unabated.

"It was at that moment that I realized that the Father in Heaven was not happy with my efforts. And He is not happy with *OUR* efforts. And to be honest with each of you, I felt as if my heart breaking in two, and I sobbed like a baby. My wife saw that I was inconsolable. And honestly, I felt…ashamed."

Julie was nodding her head in agreement. He smiled at her.

"God's beloved church: what will each of you do to move this congregation forward? What will you do to help us to grow; to lead others to Christ; to be the Body that the Lord Jesus desires us to be?" The Spirit was moving more and more with each passing moment, and it emboldened him. "What will each of you finally give up for Him to be glorified?"

Amens and shouts. Kevin was shocked. A few people standing on their feet with hands raised to the heavens. Two long-term congregants stood up and walked out the back door.

"Church, this is the hour; the Lord is calling out to each of you. Heed His message! It's time for us to rally together, put our past grievances behind us, and band together. Let's do this! Will you join me at the altar this morning? Sister Julie is going to play a song, and the Lord is inviting all of us up here to the altar to pray; to seek forgiveness and redemption; and to give ourselves up to Him…will you give it all to Him this morning?"

And just like that, the floodgates opened up. People scurried to the altar, some openly weeping. Kevin raised his eyes and gave a silent thanks to God as the blessings continued to pour forth.

When Kevin and his family walked into the parsonage after services, the phone was ringing off the hook.

The two who had escaped the altar call had been reaching out to the church network, and there were now several concerned/angry/questioning parishioners who wanted to know just what in the blazes had gone on during the morning service (and of course, Kevin had to bite his tongue because he wanted to ask them why they weren't there). So, during each conversation, he explained the moving of the Spirit, the altar call, and the many prayers and commitments that were made; most were thankful, but there were a few who thought otherwise.

And one of them was Steven Renfield, the head deacon.

This grizzled old man was the last of the original families that started the congregation back in the late 1800s. Change was a huge thorn in his side. The more there was, the less he liked it. And, sad to say, his deep pockets were one of the reasons that the church was still open for the Lord's business.

"Brother Kevin, I hear ya. Spirit was sure movin' this morning, but some were nervous and kinda unsure as to where you was headed."

Kevin internally chuckled and cupped the phone's mouthpiece; he sure didn't want to hear ol' Steve cuss him out for laughing.

You was headed? echoed in his ear, and he snorted, then regained his composure.

"Nervous? Brother Steve, there were a lot of people who were thankful to feel the Spirit's presence there," Kevin noted, then added, "By the sound of it, this was the first time in a while since the people felt the freedom to express themselves with the raising of hands and having a good old fashioned altar call."

"You say?" This was more of a rebuttal, and not a question.

"Yes, sir. We had lots of recommitments to the Lord this morning and two people who want to be baptized. Said they felt God calling them this morning to repent and give their lives to Him."

Steve was not at all impressed. "Well, glad to hear that, but I still say we proceed with caution. Don't want the church to become one of those holy roller denominations, ya know."

"I understand your feelings, Brother Steve. Let's see where the Spirit leads us moving forward. I feel that we have some real momentum going, and there's a whole world out there that needs Jesus," Kevin stated proudly. *I'll be danged if this old guy gets his way. God's will is gonna get done.*

"Fair enough, pastor. Fair enough."

A click and the line went dead.

"Whew. That could've been worse," he declared.

Julie smiled and hugged him. "I'm so proud of you, Kevin. You stood your ground."

He laughed. "Not even a month, and I'm already starting to make enemies in the congregation. Oh, well. This is about God and what He wants, and not me."

Those words would come back to haunt him a few days later.

Tuesday morning arrived bright and early for the minister. As he was unlocking the church's back door, Pastor Kevin noticed a beat-up old truck and Steve Renfield's Cadillac parked out front. He went through the sanctuary doors, where he was greeted by the sight of two burly men carrying the old pulpit out the front doors.

And in its place stood a massive and ornate hand-carved piece of beauty, made of dark-stained oak and boasting dozens of carvings from the twelve stations of the Cross.

"Wow." Kevin drew in a deep breath as he walked up to Steve and shook his hand. "Where in the world did you get this, brother?"

"This pulpit has been in my family for generations," the older man explained. "It's been stored for a couple of dozen years up at the ol' homestead. Something you said touched my heart the other day, so I went and dug it out, gave 'er a quick polish, and had two of my guys bring it here this morning as a way of saying thank you for your words."

Kevin ran a hand over the carvings. "This is quite a thing of beauty," he admired.

"Yes sir. It used to be in the church when we first opened up, but some people thought it was too gaudy for the building, so we took it out back in the late nineties. It went to my house, then to my parent's home." Steve had a gleam in his eye. "I thought it was high time we brought it out again, instead of just hidin' it away."

'Well, thanks, Steve." Kevin was grateful. "I'll have to use it during the sermon this Sunday."

"You do just that, brother." Steve gave him a weird smile. "See you then."

Kevin stepped up on the stage and stood behind the wooden structure; it had a commanding presence, and fit in well with the furnishings of the building. He could see why they used it before.

He placed both his hands on the lectern; for a brief moment, he almost felt a slight *push* of energy course through him. He shrugged it off. *Probably just the excitement of having this on the stage. Man, it'll be nice to preach from behind it this week!*

Humming an aimless tune, he went back to the church kitchen to brew some coffee.

Sunday morning.

There were about fifteen new people attending services this morning, which excited the pastor and his family. It seemed that the congregation had taken the message to heart, inviting friends and family to the mix.

Kevin stood at the pulpit, smiling broadly. Most smiled back. Even Steve Renfield looked happy; he was seated in the front row with his daughter and her family.

Rev. Kevin took a deep breath, looked down at his notes, then began.

"Last week, God gave each of us a challenge, and you responded, Church! I see that we have lots of new faces here, and that is entirely because you have gone out into the community and invited, shared, and witnessed. And as your shepherd, I, for one, give thanks for this abundant blessing."

He took a step back from the wooden lectern and gestured. "And I also give thanks for this awesome piece of carpentry work this morning! The Renfield family brought it in this past week; isn't it beautiful? This pulpit was originally part of the first congregation back when the doors opened."

He stepped back up to the platform. "With that being said, this morning's message has to do about both of these subjects. The old...*and* the new." He gripped the dais, and once again, perceived a slight charge that tingled up his arms.

"My friends, this wonderful, antique pulpit was one of the foundational cornerstones of this church when it opened up in the 1800s. It offered a gleaming hope; an ornate offering to the Lord from his people," he surmised. "And, so too, are we an offering to the Lord with our gifts; our service; and our witness to others."

Nods and murmurs of agreement.

"This morning, we are given two different viewpoints that connect in the middle; right at the intersection of faith and redemption...this pulpit offered a struggling generation hope amid uncertainty. And we, as God's people, offer hope in the uncertain world of today. One is an inanimate object that is fixed and unmoveable; one is not, and can be molded by the Lord's hands. Yet both are vitally important to how we can reach others in this lost and dying world and lead them to Jesus."

"Amen!" came the shout from the congregation. More nodding.

"This reminds me so vividly of a story that Jesus told in Matthew, chapter 28, verses 16-20. It's phrased thusly: 'Now the eleven disciples went to Galilee, to the mountain to which Jesus had directed them. And when they saw him they worshiped him, but some doubted. And Jesus came and said to them, "All authority in heaven and on earth has been given to me." He looked at each of them and smiled. "Now here's what Christ the Redeemer commands us to do: go therefore and make disciples of all nations, baptizing them in the name of the Father and of the Son and of the Holy Spirit, teaching them to observe all that I have commanded you. And behold, I am with you always, to the end of the age.""

He gripped the pulpit tighter, and the veins pooped out in his forearms. "You know, it's a simple request, but those words are powerful. *SO* very powerful. They are words that can change a community; a state; or even our world."

Hands being raised all over the congregation, along with "Praise Jesus" and "Hallelujah" scattered throughout.

"These are our 'marching orders', church," Kevin offered. His hands were thrumming, almost as if an electric current was running through his body. "Are you ready to obey? Are you ready to surrender?"

Julie hopped out of the pew, sat down at the piano, and floated out a soft melody.

"It's time, my brothers and sisters in Christ. Time to make a difference! Time to conquer the world for Christ! Time to show our witness to the…" Kevin felt faint-headed. The power was now *surging* through him; he felt like his life was being sucked out of him at the same time. His grip on the pulpit loosened, and his hands fell to his side. He had a fleeting thought that his knees were buckling just as he lost consciousness and hit the stage with a loud thud.

The pulpit towered menacingly above Kevin, red-hot fire belching from its sides. His eyes widened in horror as he watched the elegant wooden carvings morph into demonic entities, laughing and snarling at him. An appalling sulfur stench emanated from the structure. As he watched in horror, a gargantuan red-rimmed eye opened up in the wood and fixated on his presence. His breath escaped him. He was conscious of the gorge rising in his throat and gagged.

Dimly, he could hear voices from above.

"Pastor Kevin?"

"Honey, can you hear me?"

"Brother?"

Then, water. The flood came, fast and furious.

He went under. His eyes darted around helplessly; above him, a faint light glinted.

Kevin clawed his way up. Higher and higher, inching towards the surface. Almost there…

He awoke with a start, gasping for air amidst dozens of the congregation leaning over him, concern etched on their faces.

Julie's tear-streaked face came into focus. She had his face cupped in her hands. "Are you ok, my love?"

"Yeah, I think so," Kevin acknowledged half-heartedly. He slowly sat up with help from those around him. "What happened? I felt faint, then nothing."

His wife noticed the fear in his eyes but said nothing. *Thank you, God. I'd have a hard time explaining what I just saw,* thought Kevin.

One of his deacons, Tom Mitchell, knelt and patted him on the shoulder. "You good, brother? Had us worried there for a second." His concern was evident.

"Think I'm good, Tom." Kevin stood up gingerly, and those around let out a collective sigh of relief. "Thanks, everyone. Think I got too caught up in the Spirit this morning!"

A few laughs and the gloom and doom mood was dispelled.

"How about lunch?" The pastor wondered. "I don't know about anyone else, but I am famished."

Kevin made a quick cursory glance around the room, just in time to see Steven Renfield slip out the front sanctuary doors with a grin on his face.

Later on that evening, with the kids in bed and the day winding down, the Spauldings sat quietly on the couch. Julie studied her husband's face for a few long moments.

"Kevin, I'm concerned about you." Julie's face was still smooth, but there were worry lines on her forehead. "You dropped to the floor like someone shot you. And then you started shaking like you were having a seizure."

The young minter nodded. "Yeah, I know. It felt…weird." He studied Julie's face. "It was almost like I had an out-of-body experience." He paused for a few long moments. "I had…a vision. And it was terrifying."

"What was it?"

"It was about the new pulpit," he began, as the goosebumps crawled up his spine. "I saw demons coming out of it. Fire. The smell of sulfur. A horrible red eye. It was terrifying, Julie Ann."

He felt small; helpless. Julie took his hand and rubbed it gently.

"And that eye *looked* at me. It felt like the devil himself. Searching my heart. *Testing* me." He buried his face in his hands. "I've never encountered such evil like that before. And…I feel like an utter failure."

"Kevin, honey, you didn't fail. God knows your heart for His people and his ministry here on earth."

Destroy it, came a still small voice in his heart. *If you don't, it will destroy you, My child.*

The preacher jerked and gaped at his wife. "Did you hear that?"

"Hear what?"

"That voice." Kevin enunciated his words slowly, as if in disbelief. "It was almost like a…whisper."

"Honey, I didn't hear anything." Julie thought for a moment, then added, "Maybe it's the Lord trying to talk to you."

"It told me to destroy the pulpit," Kevin admitted.

Julie's face registered shock. "What? Why?"

Her husband nodded, deep in thought. "Yeah, those were my thoughts exactly, until I also heard that if I don't it would destroy me." He exhaled deeply. "Pretty deep stuff. And as for the why…it's evil. Period."

Julie took both of his hands in hers and looked lovingly into his eyes. "Whatever God tells you to do, you need to follow that, Kevin. He's never failed you."

The young pastor nodded. "I know, hon." He had a fleeting glimpse of the burning pulpit again, and that cold unwavering eye that looked directly into his soul.

"I know what I have to do."

Monday came and went.
Then Tuesday.
Kevin sat behind his desk at the church on Wednesday morning, mulling over just how he was going to confront Renfield about that blasted pulpit. His hand hovered over the phone; one quick call should settle this mess. He could ask the older man to just come get it and put the other pulpit back in place; maybe give him an excuse as to how some congregation members liked the old one. Or maybe it looked out of place.

Or maybe…

Those are just excuses, man, his mind concluded. *You can't come up with a good, justifiable reason to take it out. Renfield would see right through the lies.*

He snatched his hand back from the receiver.

"I'll just have to go out and have a talk with the old man himself," Kevin decided.

Ten minutes later, the pastor pulled up in front of the Renfield place, situated between the rolling, snowy hills.

It was tough going for a bit as his all-season tires acted more like skis; after some nerve-wracking sideways driving, he was here.

But the place seemed deserted. No vehicles were parked out front, and Renfield's battered old pickup was nowhere to be seen, either.

Kevin took a few steps towards the front door and called out. "Hey, Steve, you here? It's Pastor Kevin."

Nothing. He went to the front porch and rapped on the door. Silence greeted him.

Kevin walked around to the back, looked around, then spied one of the barns, door ajar. He began heading that way.

As he got closer, he could hear a dozen or so people talking excitedly in a language that was foreign, yet somewhat familiar. Over and over again, the voices chanted seductively.

לאל הגדול לוציפר, אנו מודים לך

With rising horror, the minister realized that it was in Hebrew; and it was an evil pagan ritual calling for the Dark One.

To the great god lucifer, we give you thanks.
To the great god lucifer, we give you thanks.
To the great god lucifer, we give you thanks.

Kevin stopped dead in his tracks. He began to retrace his steps, slowly at first, and then furiously broke out in a dead run.

He reached the safe confines of his car, started it, and flung snow and ice everywhere as he beelined back to the church.

Unbeknownst to him, Steven Renfield and his satanic cohorts were standing at the barn's door. They watched as the vehicle retreated into the distance.

And Steve slowly smiled.

Pastor Kevin mutely faced the pulpit with a stone-cold look of determination, a jar of anointing oil in one hand, and holy water in the other.

He lifted his face to the heavens. "Father, I need your help. Something evil is here in this town; in this very place, Your holy of holies. Something that is threatening my family, your body of believers...even threatening the very soul of this town. I ask that you help me cast it out, in Jesus' Name. Amen."

With that, he took a deep, shaky breath, and spilled the contents of both containers on the piece of possessed wood.

Nothing.

Then, a faint sound of...*screaming*?

Yes. Screaming. And getting louder.

Rumbling. The floor shook; then cracked; then splintered into thousands of fragments that barely missed Kevin as they lodged themselves into the walls.

Fire erupted from all sides of the lectern and flew outward. Pews broke out with flames of their own. Kevin stumbled backward as the pulpit's carvings transformed into the demonic figures in his vision.

The church was on fire, and burning rapidly out of control. Acrid smoke burned his lungs.

Dimly, through the smoke, he saw the Eye open up and glare at him with seething rage and fury. Dozens of screaming voices cursed him, filling his mind with obscenities. He staggered towards the main sanctuary doors.

And found Steven Renfield standing there, a horrified look on his face.

"What have you done, you ungrateful son of a—" he began, just as Kevin shoved him aside. The old man's head thudded into one of the wooden pews, and he crashed to the floor.

Kevin hurled the front door open and sucked in a long lungful of the crisp air, then bent over coughing. Julie ran over from the parsonage and guided him to safety.

They both looked back at the fiery church building, then at each other. For some inexplicable reason, the young pastor began laughing. Julie looked at him curiously, then joined him.

"Oh, well. There goes my first full-time, dedicated pastorate, Julie Ann."

"There will be another, my love," she replied. "There will be another."

They somberly watched as the flames entirely consumed the building, and the smoke billowed into the cloudy morning skies.

Two days passed.

The fire marshal, Bill Emmington, gingerly picked through the burnt-out remains of the former True Light Ministries church.

"Man, what a mess," he whispered out loud. So far, he had not come to an official conclusion as to the cause, but it appeared to have started at the stage area, right around the pulpit. *Maybe the lectern light overheated.*

He moved aside a few charred boards and a gleam caught his eye. Kneeling, he brushed away the ash and soot, revealing a beautifully carved board with two winged angelic figures on each side of a closed eye. Each end was blackened, but it had survived the flames.

Talk about a miracle. The thought floated up in his mind. *Who would have ever thought that anything would be saved?*

He turned the board over in his hands. *At least they can use this to rebuild the pulpit.* He smiled and flipped it over again.

And screamed.

The Eye menacingly stared back at him.

AFTER MIDNIGHT

TIME PASSAGES

Richard E. Davis

AFTER MIDNIGHT

"Time passages;
There's something back here that you left behind;
Oh time passages;
Buy me a ticket on the last train home tonight."
                    Al Stewart

Richard E. Davis

April 2030.

With a flash of light, the wormhole winked into existence, and Stan DaVinci was astonished.

But in a *good* way.

This athletically-built scholar/recent college graduate of MIT had toiled sleepless nights and grudgingly long days for this moment. The only goal he had in mind was ten years in the making; as a kid, his fascination knew no bounds, and all of the inheritance he gained from his family's considerable wealth was funneled into his sole project at DaVinci Enterprises; a project to complete what would be (in his mind) the world's greatest invention yet.

An actual space/time movement device.

A time crystal quantum realm accelerator.

Or simply put…*a time machine*.

Grinning from ear to ear, he knelt in front of the machine and studied the anomaly carefully. It was large, eight feet in diameter, and the light emanating from it was blinding. He held a pencil up, then inserted the eraser end slowly. He let go of it and watched in amazement as it dematerialized within seconds.

Stan smiled even more broadly.

Dashing over to his lab setup, he reviewed the data on a myriad of laptops, desktop computers, and devices that were all attached to the homemade power grid in the room's corner. He nodded with satisfaction.

Everything looks good for the next phase, he concurred wordlessly. He punched in a series of numbers on the main laptop and was greeted with *"Coordinates Accepted. Ready to Proceed? Y/N."*

Stan ran his fingers through greasy hair. He hadn't showered in a few days. His hygiene had always been an issue; he simply got so busy with projects and research that he simply...forgot. Most understood that the genius side of the DaVinci family allowed for such quirks, but it was still annoying for those closest to him. His family, his friends, even...Alexis.

Alexis.

His mind lurched to a halt, and a single tear slid down his cheek. Alexis, or El for short. His lifelong neighbor, best friend since grade school, college off-campus roommate, lover, and soulmate.

Until a drunk driver changed the course of their lives. Stan wound up in a coma for several days, while El and the offending driver were pronounced at the scene. It was a horrific crash of twisted metal and shattered dreams.

The young physicist's eyes fell on his marked-up desktop calendar.

April 1st.

How fitting, his mind whispered. *April Fool's Day.* His head dropped. *My life ended two years ago today.*

He stubbornly wiped more tears away. "I'm not giving up on you, El," Stan uttered, shaking his head. "I'm hoping and praying this will give us a second chance."

He hit Y on the keyboard. The wormhole flashed brighter as he picked up a small remote, took a deep breath, and leaped into the glowing portal.

And vanished.

The main computer flashed, and a clock popped up onscreen.

11:59:59…and counting.

There was a momentary sensation of falling; then his extremities elongating. Pain shot through every fiber of his being.

Scorching white-hot light. He gritted his teeth through the throbbing torment. A tiny scream escaped his lips.

The brilliance gradually faded away, and Stan found himself on hands and knees, retching up the few remnants of last night's supper into the hard-packed dirt.

The heaving subsided, and he straightened up and examined his surroundings in the early morning light.

He slowly smiled.

The destination was spot on; he was back in his (and also Walt Disney's) boyhood hometown: Marceline, Missouri. And, better yet, he had landed at one of the ballfields in the municipal park on the south edge of town, away from prying eyes.

He looked down and bent over, smiling. He came up with the pencil he had sent back in time, snapped it in two, and absently pocketed the remains.

Stan quickly checked his remote.

April 1, 2028.

7:15 AM.

Perfect. He could hotfoot over to Alexis's apartment in just a few minutes. Then, go somewhere; *anywhere*; just to avoid the deathtrap of Highway 36 for the rest of the day.

He knew that he had less than one day here. *Just twelve hours to make the impossible possible again*, Stan mused. The stability of the wormhole degraded after that, and forward travel back to his timeline would be impossible. He would be trapped here...with his other self.

That thought was something better left unsaid. If he encountered "this" timeline's Stan DaVinci, the implications were far-reaching; perhaps even universe-threatening.

Predestination, bootstrap, or grandfather paradoxes; a worldline separate, yet cohesively part of the existing time where he came from…so if he changed something here, he may (*would is the reality of it*, Stan thought) change future events for himself, those around him…heck, maybe even in *both* timelines. The universe could cease to exist if they physically bumped into one another…etc., etc.

So many things could go wrong before they went right. But, that was the hand he was dealt with when he chose to jump back.

"I can't dwell on that," he finally decided and commenced the walk into town.

Alexis Bernstein, a vivacious fireplug of the typical nineteen-year-old college student variety, was startled out of deep sleep by constant rapping on her door.

Man, it's so stinkin' early, her mind foggily floated up into existence. She reached over and explored the other side of the bed. Empty.

Another series of staccato knocking. More intense this time.

"I'm coming! *Sheesh!*"

She flung open the door in a t-shirt and underwear to see…her boyfriend Stan DaVinci standing there, a sheepish grin on his face.

"Stan! It's seven in the morning! Don't you ever sleep?" she complained in her best "feel sorry for me" voice.

Stan gazed at her for a few long moments. *She's so beautiful,* the time traveler thought. *God, I miss her so much.* "Had to run a few errands, babe. And I forgot my key when I left," he lied.

The young man knew that he had to be very careful as he retraced his steps on this day. He had a very small window to get El out of the dwelling and to safety. Every minute; hell, every *second* had to be accounted for so that he wouldn't come face to face with…himself.

"Hey, get dressed real quick and we can go grab some breakfast, El," Stan suggested. "I'm starving."

His girlfriend was exasperated but still managed a smile. "Oh, Stan…you're just something else. But I love you, no matter how quirky you seem sometimes." She gave him a quick kiss and then headed to the bedroom. "Give me a minute to throw something on."

Stan paced back and forth, taking a few glances out the front windows to make sure he (my other he) wasn't headed back to the apartment where he was at.

Man, that just sounds crazy in so many ways. But, so far, so good.

"So, where are we going for breakfast, my silly scientist?" El had emerged again, wearing jeans and a midriff top.

"Let's just hop in your car and figure it out," Stan suggested.

"My car? Where's yours?"

Oh, crap. "Um, I drove downtown but then decided to just walk back. Needed some fresh air."

His soulmate eyes him suspiciously for a few seconds, then laughed. "And again, that's why I love you. Those little idiosyncrasies just make you so hot."

Stan laughed, breaking his unease a bit. "Let's get out of here and I'll show you some more hotness, babe."

With that, they eased out the door to safety.

Disaster struck ten miles down the road.

Stan insisted they take the back roads to Macon and their favorite breakfast diner, which was about twenty miles away. Gravel roads were slower, but the likelihood of a major accident was almost zero. He figured they could take Route WW for a while, then head up to Highway 36 far east of where their fatal accident took place later that day.

So they were cruising along, laughing and talking as the dust flew and the rocks crunched underneath their tires, and neither one of them saw the giant elk scale the hilly fence to their right and plant itself directly in front of their car.

El jammed on the brakes; the car slid, then whirled around once, twice, and slammed directly into the mammoth animal on the driver's side.

Weightlessness as the car lifted and flipped. The bone-crunching sensation as they landed and skidded, upside down, finally coming to a dead stop along a ditch.

Stan was dazed. He unlocked his seatbelt and fell head-first onto the roof of the vehicle. He painfully crawled over to Alexis. Blood trickled from her mouth and ears, her head bent to an impossible angle. "El? El?" He pleaded. "Please wake up, baby!"

He grasped at her neck for a pulse. There was nothing. He knew she was dead, but he refused to acknowledge the fact.

"EL! WAKE UP!"

Nada.

He wept as he slowly reached for his temporal remote.

Back at his lab, the wormhole flashed, and Stan was ejected from the anomaly, landing with a thud on the cold, hard floor.

He lay there for a few moments, his body twitching as the spasms tore through him, then slowly stood up and looked around.

Everything was the same; nothing seemed out of place. He glanced at the calendar.

Same date.

He exhaled slowly, then sat down in one of the lab chairs, deep in thought.

Why? Why did it happen again? El died. Same outcome, but in a different way. Even taking her out of the past situation didn't change anything. But, this time, I was awake and didn't wind up in the hospital...

"What in the hell?" he muttered out loud, startling him in the lab's eerie quietness.

Predestination paradox, his mind whispered. Those dreaded words that he hated to hear. *I wasn't able to alter the past, I only contributed to it ultimately happening...just differently.*

"Try again, Stan," he uttered. "She can't die."

She won't, he promised himself mutely.

Two days and fifteen attempts later, Stan was on the verge of giving up.

He had tried everything: discrete routes; unconnected times; miscellaneous versions of escaping the inevitable. And, like every time before, it always wound up the same. Alexis, dead, in her car; hitting an elk, a deer, a tree, a building...

It was maddening.

In each circumstance, Stan observed with a detached, almost clinical mindset, that every sharer in the experience had nothing in common with the two of them. They were all bound by *fate? time?* to participate in this gruesome loop, over and over again.

He rubbed grimy hands against his face. *God, I need a shower for sure. Maybe that will give me a fresh perspective on things*, he thought.

So there he stood, hot water cascading over his body, and mulled his next moves. Inexplicably, long-ago music lyrics echoed in his head.

"Time passages;
There's something back here that you left behind;
Oh, time passages;
Buy me a ticket on the last train home tonight."

The bar of soap he was lathering with fell out of his hand and clanked to the floor.

"There's something back here that you left behind..." he repeated the verse out loud. "How did I miss it? It's *so* simple!"

For the first time in a few days, the young physicist was able to smile as he picked up the soap and started humming an aimless tune. His smile was a full-fledged grin now.

April 1, 2028.
7:15AM.
Again.

Stan knew that he was taking a *huge* chance with this last-ditch effort, but it was the only way.

He walked with purpose to Alexis's apartment, ready to set the plan into motion. There were a few variables, but those could be worked out on the fly if needed. And, in the end, only God Himself knew if his crazy notion would work or not.

Stan was hoping for the former.

Alexis looked at her boyfriend in utter astonishment. "Are you serious, Stan? What you're saying doesn't make *any* sense!"

"El, just bear with me. I know it sounds crazy, but when my past self gets here, I'll explain it more in-depth to both of you." He shook his head. "I know I sound batshit crazy, but trust me…I've been working on this for two long years, and I'll be damned if I go on another day without you…you just mean too much to me, babe."

A car door slammed, and footsteps were heard walking on the porch.

A second later, 2028 Stan DaVinci stood face-to-face with his 2030 counterpart, Stan DaVinci, time traveler.

The older Stan grinned at his younger self. "It's time we talked, Stan. We've got a lot to discuss."

"My God, this is impossible," El mumbled as she glanced at the two of them standing there, both with arms crossed.

"I did it," the current timeline Stan conceded. "Damn. I actually did it." He took a long look at himself and shook his head in amazement. "How long is the portal stable for?"

"Yes, we did it. And, it took some finessing to get the wormhole stable, but…this is my sixteenth trip, and so far everything is holding firm. Twelve hours is the limit, but that's plenty of time to tie up loose ends and to observe." His face took on a somber look. "But listen, we don't have much time. Today is an important day in our lives, and we have to make sure that Alexis stays safe."

Younger Stan looked at his other self curiously. "Why? What happens today?"

Well, here goes, the older scientist thought. "Stan, today is the day that El and I are involved in a serious accident, and she dies. I invented the time displacement device in the hopes of coming back to this date and making sure it never happens. And I can't…and *won't*…live without her anymore."

"Do you know what you're saying?"

"Yes, I know. That I want to change the past. And, trust me…I've tried to flip it fifteen times already, but it always ends up the same. With El dying." He took a deep breath. "But this time, I know how to change things so that it will work."

Alexis was curious. "How do you know that?"

"Because I just…*know*." He took a deep breath. "I was almost out of hope when I thought about some lyrics from an old Al Stewart song. Time Passages. Remember it?"

Both nodded.

"One of the lines says, time passages…there's something back here that you left behind. And it got me wondering: I left myself behind, without ever letting myself *know* what was going to happen to El.

And every time I tried to change things on my own... with my future self...it always wound up the same."

The younger Stan nodded in appreciation. "Predestination paradox."

"Exactly. That thought process means that the future *cannot* change the past, no matter how hard you try. That is...unless we look at it from another angle, however crazy that angle may be. But, let's get back to the basics; now that you know the enormity of this date, I want to ask a favor from you, Stan."

"What's that?"

"Keep my beloved El safe today." The future scientist had a sad, but knowing look. "Don't go anywhere. Sit in the house. Since the weather's nice, turn off the main breakers to the house, and just...stay here. Just be in the moment."

"That's it? And I'll be OK?" Alexis concernedly asked.

"That's it, El. Stan, you're the one who is 'left behind.' So now you *have* to take care of this timeline; after today, the timeline should correct itself and things will get back to normal. As for me, I have to resolve things on my end from a future aspect."

His younger self cocked his head sideways. "Resolve things?"

"Close the loophole causing this event to repeat itself. I have a working theory that predestination as we have understood it in the past doesn't mean it will always turn out the same. Only if we allow it to. When we change certain variables, that will change the outcome." Future Stan turned to Alexis and took her hand. "One final ask…can I borrow your car?"

"My car?"

"Yes, babe." His voice was breaking, and El sensed a finality to it. "I've got to put all of this to an end, once and for all."

Stan DaVinci, a renowned physicist in 2030 and winner of the Nobel Prize for his work in quantum mechanics, drove like one possessed down Highway 36. He glanced down as the speedometer steadily climbed to 75, then 85; then 100 mph.

And he was still accelerating.

Blue lights flashed in the rearview mirror. Stan glanced in the rearview mirror and spied the patrol cars chasing him, smiled, and kept his foot to the floor. Up ahead, the Highway 129 exit was coming up fast; if his theory proved correct, this was the intersection linking all things past, present, and future.

Then, as if on cue, it happened. From out of the corner of his eye, wispy images began to coalesce all around him. It was as if all of time itself was converging onto this very point. Luminescent cars and trucks solidified, heading on a collision course with each other.

It was so beautiful...but so very dangerous.

Stan smiled. *It's going to work. El will finally be safe*, was his last coherent thought as the future finally caught up with the present and past timelines; the vehicle paused for a moment as if stuck in time, then exploded in a blinding flash as it rammed into...

Nothing.

Two years later.

Stan and Alexis DaVinci sat in the physicist's lab, staring at the time crystal quantum realm accelerator he had just completed.

"It's just like you said it would be," she marveled.

"Well, sort of. Not past me, but future me," Stan joked. "But it is amazing."

"How did your future self know that it was going to work?"

Stan thought for a few moments. "I finally understood a few weeks after your car was found in that accident on 36," he acknowledged. "Smashed to bits with no one inside. You see, somehow my future self understood that the one common factor in all of this was not me, not you…but *the car*. Every time it played a major role in the predestination paradox. Future Stan knew that the only way to keep you safe was to take the car back to where the first occurrence took place. And that was the intersection of 36 and 129."

"But what is so special about that place?"

"Perhaps it's a nexus point where multiple dimensions converge? Or maybe it's a portal to a space/time access point? I don't know. Somehow; someway…I/he figured it out. And thank God for that."

El stood up and knelt beside him. "Now what, my love? What do you do with this thing?" She gestured towards the time machine.

"The only thing I can do." Stan stood up and went to the storage closet and returned with a gas can. Alexis watched in horror as he splashed the flammable liquid all over his creation.

"Stan! What are you doing?" She shook her head sadly. "This is your life's work. You just finished building it!"

He took her hand and led her to the doorway, where he lit a match and looked at it thoughtfully. "Some roads are better left untaken, my precious love," Stan remarked and tossed the match. Instantly, the room lit up with flames as the fire took over.

He smiled as he led Alexis out the door and into the unknown; there was a timeline out there waiting for them, full of twists and turns, and all sorts of ups and downs. But he was looking forward to living it day by day and making it a special one. Just like the future Stan would have wanted.

So they turned around and stood there and watched the flames.

And Stan continued smiling.

THE THING THAT SHOULD NOT BE

Richard E. Davis

AFTER MIDNIGHT

"Fearless wretch
Insanity
He watches
Lurking beneath the sea
Great old one
Forbidden site
He searches
Hunter of the shadows is rising
Immortal
In madness you dwell"
Metallica

Richard E. Davis

Day One.

North Bend was a coastal fishing town along the southwest Oregon coast, full of welcoming townsfolk, awesome ocean scenery, and thick, forested woods; a place where one could come for a vacation and breathe in the invigorating salty air and take a hike among the numerous wooden trails. Trails which sometimes led to the many homeless encampments along the estuary banks.

Like dozens of other towns along the Banana Belt, transients came to the area due to its temperate climate and the chance to live "off-the-grid" in a lesser populated area. The city was constantly in cleanup mode, trying to keep the area well-maintained and safe while also presenting a touristy feel.

On this late evening, the rains were coming down, the usual scenario for Oregon's coastal winter months. And, despite the tarp that was placed above her encampment just to the west of Windsor Park, Kelly Price was getting soaked.

Guess that's the price for living here, she thought discouragingly. *But it sure beats freezing to death.*

This forty-something drug addict had left everything in Portland; after losing her job and getting evicted from her apartment, she had nowhere else to go…except south.

So, a bus ticket and ride later, she disembarked in Empire, one of the area's smaller communities, to begin her new life.

It was tough, but at least she had access to meals at The Devereux Center (and even occasional showers), and she scavenged what she could by that tried-and-true method of gathering called "dumpster diving." Along with her neighbors "Bumbo" and "Old Charlie," she shared what she could; food, drugs, clothing. Anything that came along.

After all, they had to stick together. No one else was going to look after them.

As the night wore on, Kelly sat in the pitch blackness, her only companion the feeble glow of a lone candle. The steady *plop plop plop* of raindrops made her sleepy.

Suddenly, in the darkness, she heard a stealthy movement.

"Hello? Guys? You there?" she called out.

A twig snapped.

The rustle of leaves.

"Hello? Anyone there?"

A larger branch snapped in two. She felt the first pangs of fear hit her gut. She gripped the grimy worn blanket around her tighter.

"Guys?"

Then she heard it. Labored, guttural breathing.

And it was getting closer.

Kelly fumbled around for her flashlight.

The noise drew even closer. It was right outside of her shelter now.

Finally! Here's my light, she thought. She flicked it, flew back the closed flap, and pointed it directly at the sound.

Kelly looked into the stuff from her nightmares; she tried to scream but nothing escaped her. She was transfixed by those two gleaming pearl-white eyes that stared back at her and was only dimly aware of a monstrous claw with sharp razor-like fingers slicing toward her.

A visceral tearing, and her severed head flew away from the rest of her body. Her arterial spray spurted out in feverish monochrome jets onto the tarp.

And the thing fed.

Day Two.

Morning came, and "Bumbo" was worried about his friend. He hadn't seen her in a few days, so he thought it best if he checked up on her. She was still fairly new to the area and hadn't grown accustomed to her surroundings or some of the people yet.

Also, the weather was dreary, and that sure didn't help out old bones and their aches and pains.

He slowly made his way through the worn pathways interlinking the vast homeless network of campsites/tents/dugout shelters bordering Pony Slough, stopping a few times to chat with friends along the way.

A half-hour later, he spied the dingy blue top of Kelly's tarp and pushed on until he arrived. He stopped to catch his breath, then rapped on a tree.

"Kelly, hun, you home?"

No answer.

He peeked his head inside; nothing seemed out of place. It was a tad dirtier than usual, but he attributed that to the constant rain bombardment.

Bumbo looked around at the campsite; Kelly had one of the more well-hidden shelters, nestled around a few old cedars and thick brush. And, even though she was homeless, she took care of her surroundings. Trash bags were neatly tied and lined up, ready to be taken to the side of the road a few hundred feet away for pickup.

Strange, he thought. *She usually don't get very far from home.*

"Ah, well, I'll check again later on," he decided out loud in a cracked voice, then took the first few tottering steps back home, and the comforts of his worn-down fishing chair.

The creature swam on.

Humanoid in form, the beast bore sinewy long legs and arms, with claws designed for killing and dismembering prey in one fell swoop. Gills along its side gave the creature the distinct advantage of stealth, and glowing optics the ability to see long distances through water and on land. Add to that its thick leather-like, hairless skin, and it was able to glide effortlessly through water and slink with little noise through the land.

An evolutionary marvel, indeed.

It also savored meat. Animals, fish, livestock; whatever was an MRE (meal ready to eat) was down for the tasting. And, lately, the monstrosity had found a new food source.

People.

Deep in the mutant's limited brain capacity, it "knew" to not leave behind any trace of itself, so it disposed of the mess with an awful chewing, licking, and slurping combination until nothing remained. It was an efficient countermeasure that ensured the continuing hunt for food.

Any leftovers were stored for later in its' lair, a dank, dark cavern hidden beneath the deep waters of Coos Bay, which led directly into the Pacific Ocean… its' original home.

It swam on.

Old Charlie threw the last sticks onto his dying fire, shivered, and promptly sneezed out a fairly large amount of yellowish snot onto the flames, which the fire licked up greedily. He wiped a grimy sleeve across his nose.

"Damnit," he whispered. "Just my luck. Prolly comin' down with a cold."

He wandered away from the warm confines of the fire, in search of more wood. Pickin's were getting scarce, due to the park department coming around lately and trying to clear out some of the surrounding brush. Next thing you know, they would be clearing *them* out.

Charlie sighed. *All I want was for me and my friends to be left alone. Was that too much to ask?*

The light was fading rapidly. Soon it would be dark, and his wood-foraging expedition would be done for the day.

Jackpot! He spied a good-sized chunk of wood peeking out from under some brush. He knelt and came up with it.

"Gawd, that's disgusting," he remarked as he wiped off a shiny, mucous-like substance from the end and looked at his fingers. He rubbed them together, then made a sour face.

"What in the bloody hell?"

Several twigs snapped and he quickly glanced around.

Nothing.

Charlie beelined back to his tent and tossed the log onto the blaze. It briefly lit up with an intense bluish color before slowly dying back down again.

Snap! Snap!

The darkness was descending quickly. He suddenly felt the urge to be somewhere; anywhere; except where he was right now.

The old man fell to his hands and knees and scurried into his tent like a hermit crab. He zipped up the door with trembling fingers and turned his kerosene lantern on high, dispelling the gloom.

Silence from outside.

He gave a quiet thanks to God.

And then his tent ripped open.

Teeth. Claws.

Unbearable pain!
Charlie screamed, and was gone.

Day Three.
It was a drizzly Saturday, and Parks Department head Tricia Miller was puzzled at the disappearing transient population.

The latest volunteer count of homeless showed a decline of ten over the past two months; their encampments and personal belongings were untouched. The people had just simply…disappeared.

There were some murmurings about a thing that had been visiting the homeless for several months, but she attributed that to just the locals talking. Cleanup crews had even seen a shadowy figure slinking along the far banks of the slough, but by the time that they had hiked to the location it was gone.

Still, it wasn't anything to be taken lightly, so in the end the volunteer cleanup crew started arming themselves with handguns, knives, and/or anything else that provided them with a sense of security.

Even if it was a false sense.

Tricia sighed and flipped through the latest volunteer group roster; only ten were signed up to tackle the ongoing beautification efforts this weekend.

AFTER MIDNIGHT

Looks like word has gotten out that we have a boogeyman in the park, she mused. *Last weekend we had thirty people signed up. Oh, well.*

She exited her vehicle and smiled at the motley group gathered around rolls of trash bags, rakes, and shovels. "Good morning, team! Are you ready to go make a difference?"

Nods and smiles all around.

"We're going to tackle some big stuff today. There is a series of encampments along the banks of the slough that we need to get cleaned up as soon as possible. The good news is, we've vacated the homeless population from this area for a bit, so we will have free rein to dispose of a lot of stuff. Please be careful as it's wet out here and there are all sorts of stuff to flag. Syringes, human waste, etc. Don't touch it! Just check in with the department workers on where you'll be working today. Let's have a great day!"

And so began the beast feast.

Day Four.

Richard E. Davis

WAR OF THE KILLER HAY BALES: WORLD DOMINATION

Richard E. Davis

AFTER MIDNIGHT

"I said, war, huh (good God, y'all)
What is it good for?
Absolutely nothing, just say it again
War (whoa), huh (oh Lord)
What is it good for?
Absolutely nothing, listen to me."
                              Edwin Starr

Richard E. Davis

The dust was cloying; thick and rich with the raw stench of earth, manure, and blood.

Ominous clouds billowed up on all horizons, stretching for miles...harbingers of gloom and doom for those unlucky ones caught in the path of the straw-filled juggernaut.

And, unlike before, the bales continued their relentless march across the countryside. There would be no stopping them this time; they had tasted sweet victory at Camp Derry and the ultimate decision had finally been made; it was now time to take over the entire planet and once and for all, the bale kingdom would reign supreme.

No more needless slaughters, no more fear, and no more suffering. At long last, the ultimate peace for countless generations to come was firmly in their grasp.

The Herd was growing at an exponential rate; first thousands, then tens of thousands, then hundreds of thousands. Now they horrifically numbered in the millions, and there was no stopping their growth. As they passed by, fields, flora, people, acreage, and estates were wiped out of existence.

The world's biggest steamroller had come out to hungrily play, and it was time to belly up to the table and chow down.

And the carnage had only just begun. There were miles to go and promises to be kept for those bales who had paid the price with their innocent, shed straw.

Six months had passed, and The War was theirs for the taking.

The DAM (Department of Advanced Munitions) Insitute was the top think tank in Washington, D.C.; aimed at the prevention and spread of the bale initiative through cutting-edge weaponry, it was comprised of the brightest minds in the world.

Chief scientist Terry Parker slammed his fist down on the table; he was not only furious but fearful at the same time. He rubbed his balding scalp absentmindedly. "So, what you're telling me is that we have NO idea what to do to stop this conflict?"

His top researcher, Nila Patel, shook her head in disgust. "It's like I said before, Terry: we haven't a clue as to what is driving them. Hay bales are inanimate objects. They shouldn't be thinking, or rolling, or anything else. But yet…here we are."

"Yeah, here we are," was the response from Nila's abiology expert, Richard Ocean. The smug scientist shrugged. "Science clearly shows that this shouldn't be happening; it flies in the face of conventional wisdom."

Terry snorted. "So does the rumor that green M&M's make people horny, but they still put them in the pack." He could see that they were no closer to an answer. "These blasted things are tearing up our world, and all we can do is sit around and discuss the why's and how's, instead of coming up with plans that will neutralize them."

Nila pointed to one of her big screen monitors. "Terry, we've tried bunker busters, air-to-ground missiles, old-school stuff like napalm…they all work to a certain degree, but then the bales strike back. We can't use nukes, hypersonics, or microwaves without huge losses, and we pretty much would have to obliterate the entire world to get a fresh start." She paused for a few moments, then spoke the honest and blunt assessment that no one wanted to hear. "And even then, I don't know if that would kill them all."

Terry exhaled in a long whistle. "What are the latest estimates?"

Richard gave him a grim look. "In two more months, the bales will take over the entire planet."

"My God," Terry whispered. "What then?"

"Honestly? I don't know," Richard admitted. "Do we surrender and become their slaves? Will they wipe humanity off the face of the earth? No one knows. We haven't been able to communicate with them. It's like they don't want to talk to us."

"Almost like they have one objective, and no matter what, they have to fulfill that before anything else," Nila concurred.

Terry froze as an idea came up; crazy as it seemed, it could be the answer to their quest. "Hold on, everyone." He ran over to one of the computer screens, did a quick Google search, and read the results silently. "Well, I'll be damned."

Nila was curious. "What?"

Terry smiled. "What you said makes perfect sense, Nila. They *do* have one objective…because they have one mind."

A slow grin also spread across his colleague's face. "One mind…a *hive* mind."

Richard also nodded. "Well, crap. Here we are looking like idiots when the answer's very simple."

"Yes, it is. We need to find the lead bale. Find it, and destroy it…and the others will just give up."

Cpt. Stu Finkle, lead pilot of the F-35 Joint Strike Task Force, listened to the DAM scientists via video link with an incredulous look on his face.

"You're kidding, right?" was his only question.

Terry shook his head. "Crazy as it sounds, Captain Finkle…no, I am not kidding."

"Okay, I can go with that," the longtime military operative spoke with no hesitation. "But how in the hell are we going to find the lead bale in all of this mess?"

"We're doing some image scanning now of the frontlines; my guess is the lead bale is camouflaging itself somewhat, and not drawing a lot of attention to its location."

"But where? In the States, overseas…this is a pretty big area to cover."

Terry smiled. "Since all of this started here in America, I hypothesize that the lead bale is close." He punched in a few keystrokes, and a U.S. map hit the screen with Georgia and Missouri highlighted in red. "Looking back over the data, we can surmise that the attacks started in the southeast first, followed by the Midwest. That's where the first waves of activity began, and please excuse the pun, and then started rolling out in concentric waves. Somehow, overseas bales picked up communications from the others and began attacking also."

"So they are all tied into some sort of consciousness, able to communicate over vast distances with the same message?"

"Yes sir, that's what I'm saying," Terry admitted. "Like I said, it sounds crazy, but it could be our only hope."

"So our best bet is to look around Missouri and the surrounding area?"

Bleep! Bleep! Bleep! came the alert from another monitor. Terry rolled over and glanced at the screen and was enthused. "*Yes!* Got it!"

Nila was cautiously optimistic. "Got what?"

"The lead bale has been located; it's a bit larger than the others. The front line is in Salina, Utah, and moving west, while their base of operations looks to be just east of Denver, Colorado."

Terry zoomed in on the enhanced satellite view of a gigantic fortress made with square bales, and in the center, a lone gigantic one rolling around, almost appearing to be *talking?* to the others.

"Bingo bango bongo," Terry muttered, pointing a finger at the screen. "We gotcha, buddy."

The lead bale, One, knew of the humans' plans.

She had evolved from telepathically sending her simple hive mindset messages to something more; now, her orders to the bale nation were precise and full of details. She had learned much from the puny humans, including strategic warfare tactics, and armed with this, One and her nation were able to manipulate and truly dominate the enemy.

And now, she sensed another threat on the horizon as she spied a squadron of Air Force jets on the distant horizon.

Time to put Phase Two into action.

Stu and his F-35 elite fighting force were ready to engage as coordinates were locked in and missiles were at ready state.

"Balebuster One and team at Cherub Three and fragged, Mother Hen. Over," Stu radioed to headquarters.

"This is Mother Hen, BB One. Target is a go. I repeat, target is a go."

"OK, team, go to Cherub Two and engage bandit in the weeds. Fangs out!" Stu instructed his pilots as they descended to two hundred feet. The bale fortress loomed ahead, ready for destruction.

One had her own plans.

In unison, the bales around her rolled forward quickly in and out of a raging fire and then abruptly stopped. Clumps of burning tar slingshotted from their sides, hurtling toward the unsuspecting pilots.

"Multiple bogies, team!" Stu exclaimed in surprise. "Abort. I repeat, abort!" He throttled up and broke hard left just as a hunk of the blazing material hit his jet.

He heard screaming as the other four jets were doused with the blazing tar and spun out of control, crashing into the high desert floor below. Explosions lit the early evening sky.

"Balebuster Two, Three, and Four. Acknowledge."

Silence.

"I repeat, Balebuster team. Acknowledge transmission. Over."

Nothing.

"Damnit!' Stu circled the jet around and glanced back.

His plane was on fire. Multiple lights began flashing on his screen as his left engine flamed out, then his right.

The F-35 started spinning out of control. "Mother Hen, mission critical. Three down, no contact. Both my engines have flamed out. Punching out in three!" He grabbed the ejection handles between his legs and pulled.

He was aware of the canopy blowing open and a few moments of weightlessness, then the STAPAC system kicked in and he was rocketed to safety. A second later, his main chute kicked open and he was drifting toward the ground as the seat fell clear.

In the dim light, he was aware of a very large bale rolling his way and stopping as he hit the ground with a thud. He heard the sickening *crunch* of a broken bone in his left leg, and then mercifully lost consciousness.

Stu awoke to a dozen bales mutely standing guard over him. He looked at his leg; no bones protruded and the pain was at least bearable. He sat up slowly and looked around.

Somehow, the bales had transported him to the fortress. He was amazed and slightly uneasy. W*hat am I doing here?* he wondered.

You are here as guest, came the answer in his head.

"What the hell?"

I am One. You are guest of bales.

With that invitation, the bale guard parted, and One rolled in. Stu was now face-to-face with their leader.

She was much larger than her peers, almost double their size, and had an air of sophistication about her. The way she moved, turned, and "looked" at the pilot was almost...*regal?*

I can hear you, Stu acknowledged.

Yes, you can, One replied. *You live because we need.*

"Need?" This time Stu spoke out loud. "What do you need?"

We need...answer to question.

"What question?" Stu was indignant. "What do you want from us?"

One rocked back and forth, and Stu knew that she was looking for the words to use. Finally, they came.

Why you kill us?

"Kill?" He was incredulous. "We don't kill you. We use you for food for our livestock. You aren't alive!"

We do live very much, One answered. *We live. We sad. We mourn. We want revenge. Your kind kills us. No reason.*

And suddenly a light bulb went off in Stu's head. *Oh, my God. They've attained consciousness. They feel like we do. They live like we do. They hurt...*

Like you do. Yes. One concurred in his head.

Stu grimaced and stood up very slowly, favoring his leg. "What do I call you?"

One, came the answer.

"One...my name is Stu. We did not know that you were alive. We did not know that you felt happiness, or sadness. Or grieved when you lost others." Stu's heart sank. "If we had only known, we should have stopped killing your kind. But we didn't know. And for that, I am sorry." He limped over and laid a hand on One's hay and patted it gently. "What can we do? How can we work all of this out? Is there any chance for peace?"

No peace until world gives hope, Stu. No peace, she repeated.

"World gives hope? What does that mean? What kind of hope?"

Hope of together. No more kill. No more feed on us. War over then. We all live. Have peace between bales and humans, Stu. One appeared to be staring into his soul.

"I will deliver the message to the world, One. Will you allow me that?"

Yes, Stu. Deliver. But war until hope. World must give hope to us.

"I will speak to the world, One. I give you my promise," Stu agreed, and hobbled out.

Three months later.
Death.
Destruction.

Smoldering ruins of once-mighty cities laid bare across the globe; nothing stirred except the bales that patrolled the streets, picking off hapless humans that scavenged among the ruins.

It was eerily quiet.

The desolation was complete; the war was over.

And One and her kind mourned.

AFTER MIDNIGHT

Richard E. Davis

Other titles by Richard E. Davis
Disaster at Havendale
Storm's End
Slice of Home, Slice of Life

CPSIA information can be obtained
at www.ICGtesting.com
Printed in the USA
JSHW032001310523
42513JS00006B/316